I0547080

WOUNDED

SCARRED: BOOK 2

TT KOVE

ARCTIC CIRCLE PRESS

*T*hree years on, and I'd accomplished nothing but failure.

Everyone else was getting somewhere in their lives, but I was still here, stamping in the same old shit I'd been dealing with for so long.

Three failed educations, three years of failing to keep myself harm-free, three years of failing to be healthy enough to keep myself out of hospital. The only thing I hadn't failed at was keeping my relationship intact, though that was a struggle sometimes too.

If it hadn't been for Damian and his unending patience, I would've wrecked it a long time ago. That was me, or my disorder, *something*. I wrecking every-

thing. Reacted to everything with feelings that were far too over-the-top.

But Damian was patient, and that... that was the only thing I had. Him. *Us*.

The rest of it... all a failure. *I* was a failure.

I couldn't even write. The document was glaringly white on the screen in front of me. My fingers hovered over the keyboard, unable to press down on the keys to type the words that wouldn't come to mind.

There wasn't a point in sitting there when I couldn't get anything done.

A sigh escaped as I shut the laptop, effectively putting it to sleep. I should go to sleep too. It was late.

Damian had gone to bed hours ago.

I'd stayed up because I'd wanted to write some, and because I'd been convinced I couldn't sleep yet. It was better to lay awake in bed in the dark, though, then sit there and stare at a white, glaring screen.

I went to close the curtains on the living room windows. I liked having them closed when it was dark out, but I'd forgotten to close them earlier in the evening.

Someone's out there.

The thought struck me as I stood in front of the

windows, my hands hesitating on the curtains as I peered out into the darkness

Someone stood there, I could make out the black human shape against the dark night.

Looking in our window?

Cold trickled down my spine, chilling me, making sure fear well and truly implemented itself in me.

I jerked the curtains closed. They were thick and heavy, so no one could look inside now. I hurried over to the door to check it was locked, just in case. Not that I thought someone would break in.

Or would they?

Something itched at the back of my neck, the hairs stood on end, like someone was there, watching me. The curtains were drawn now though, and I knew I was the only one awake in the flat, so it wasn't possible. Still, the body felt what the body felt, and it spooked me.

I peeked out the peep-hole, but the hallway outside was empty. One would need a key to get in the front door, so there wasn't just this one in the way of a possible burglar, but *two*.

I inched my way past the living room windows again, debating taking another peek outside, but if the black shape was still there I didn't want to know.

Instead I shut off the lights, grabbed my laptop and headed into the bedroom.

Damian was sleeping on his stomach, facing the wall. That was usually my side of the bed, but when I wasn't in it he always seemed to gravitate to my side. It was sweet, but it also left me feeling guilty because I should've been in bed with him. He had long days at school, and we spent time together when he came home, but I should also go to bed with him, keep him company until he fell asleep.

I perched on his side, and put my laptop on the nightstand, next to Damian's phone. I fluffed up his pillow before laying down, curling up on my side facing him. I couldn't see him in the dark, but just knowing he was there, breathing next to me, was enough to relax me.

But it didn't help in calming down my mind. That dark human-shaped form outside... I was certain it had looked in *our* window, but then again... our flat wasn't the only flat in the building. Not to mention the buildings on both sides.

He could've been looking in on any of them—if indeed there even had been someone out there.

Reaching out, I put my hand on Damian's back, feeling the warmth coming from him. It rose and fell slightly as he breathed. I wasn't good by myself, but with him there next to me I was stronger. Mentally anyway, but to me that was the strength that counted. It wasn't like I had that much upper body physical strength—making sure I was doing okay mentally was a lot more important than buffing up at the gym.

Damian had to be up early for school, so I didn't want to wake him by scooting in closer. He wasn't the heaviest sleeper, it didn't take all that much to wake him up. Thankfully he never tended to wake up when I went to bed late, but I kept my distance when I crawled in next to him in the middle of the night.

I love him.

That was the only thing that was clear to me.

A big part of my personality disorder was intense, problematic relationships. But him... Three years now, and he was as patient now as he'd been back when we met. Without that patience... I really would have wrecked us a long time ago. Like all other parts of my life were wrecked.

But not him. At least I had him.

PART I
PARANOIA

Noun.

Baseless or excessive suspicion of the motives of
others.

CHAPTER 1

" *M* mmm."

I woke up feeling warm and good and safe. Damian was behind me, chest close to my back and with one hand thrown over my hips.

His breathing wasn't the deep one of sleep anymore, so I could tell he was awake. As I stretched my legs out. His arm pulled me in tighter so he could hug me close.

"Feel good?" He asked, voice still rough from sleep, so he couldn't have been awake for long.

"Yeah." I sighed contently. He was all warm and hard and breathing against me, and nothing made me feel more content than that. Nothing could really compare to the time we spent in bed like this, spooning, hugging, resting, whatever… not even my messed-up mind could ruin this.

He wasn't entirely awake though, as evidenced from the way his breathing started to deepen again. He was falling back asleep.

I lifted my head a bit to look over my shoulder at him. His eyes were closed, black hair ruffled. *So peaceful.*

I stroked my palm over his arm, smiling. He had no trouble going to sleep, whereas I, when I was first awake, couldn't go back to sleep again if my life depended on it. Or like at night, when I simply couldn't go to sleep at all for no apparent reason.

I kissed his cheek, got a low sound in return, then I slid out of bed. I tried my best not to bother him. It was still early, and in a little while he had to head to school, but until his alarm started blaring I'd let him sleep.

After a hot shower, brushing my teeth and dressing in comfortable clothes, I headed into the kitchen. I had lunch with Mum today, but considering how early I was up, I could just as well have a good breakfast too.

Another thing I hadn't failed at. Well, not much anyway. I had a healthier diet nowadays than I'd had back before I met him. Healthier as in eating regularly—it wasn't like I was eating a lot of greens and whole grains.

I wasn't the best cook either, so that might have a lot to do with it. Breakfast ended up being just toast, like usual, but it was nourishment at least. I was still thin, but I'd gained some weight and muscle tone in the three years that had gone by since my stepfather had finally been put away. Since I'd met Damian.

I was on the sofa, the telly on low sound, and only halfway through my toast when Damian came out of our bedroom. He gave me a sort of half-wave before disappearing into the bathroom.

I nibbled some more on my toast and switched channels. It was too early to find anything worth watching.

Now he was up though, I could go pick up my laptop, which I'd forgot to take with me when I left the bedroom.

The telly was off and the laptop open—still on that damned white, empty page—when Damian emerged freshly showered and groomed from the bathroom.

"Morning." He sat down beside me and leaned over to kiss my cheek.

My lips instantly tipped up into a smile. "Good morning." I leaned into him, resting my head against his. "Do you have another long day ahead?" He always had nowadays.

"Yeah." His sigh was heavy. "I like it, but… it's exhausting."

"I can only imagine." I really couldn't. I'd failed the two attempts at education I'd started since I met him, and *those* hadn't been near the kind of course load he had. University degree education wasn't for me. I'd managed to finish my A-levels with just passable grades, but further than that… I always ended up in hospital. The stress, the expectations… it was too much. I couldn't handle it. And if I couldn't handle school, then what *could* I handle?

"What're your plans for the day?"

"Lunch with Mum. Other than that…" I shrugged. When did I ever have plans, besides lunches with Mum and therapy? Both single and group therapy. I was mostly quite busy, come to think of it. It was certainly more than enough for me to deal with.

He nudged me and when he managed to move his arm he put it around my shoulders. "When I get home tonight, we can do something special together. Go out for dinner, or order in. Just you and me."

"What about Silver and Kian?" Surely they would be home too.

"Silver said something about dinner with Vincent yesterday."

Right, Vincent. Silver's brother and my psychologist. The world had some funny coincidences sometimes.

"That sounds nice." Spending some good quality time with him, just the two of us, was a wonderful thing. I lived for those moments, every moment with him—it was the only part of my life that made any sense.

My gaze fell on the curtains, still drawn over the living room windows. Had there really been someone out there last night? It seemed a bit silly now, in the morning, in the daylight. But my feelings weren't something I could control. I knew they were unstable though, so I probably *had* imagined it.

I hoped.

IT WAS a crisp spring morning outside, but dark, heavy skies in the distance promised there'd be rain eventually. Not that that was unusual—we lived in London, after all.

The streets of Soho stretched out in every direction, and I took the one leading to *Harriet's Café*. For three years now, ever since I'd met Damian, it had been our usual place for lunch.

It was also where Mum had met Harriet—a wiser choice in partner than Andrew had ever been. She was sweet, kind, and obviously adored Mum. She'd never use her just so she could get to mum's kid—*me* —to abuse and do with as she wished. That was all Andrew, that sick tosser.

But I didn't want to think about him.

My mind went to really dark places when it came to him.

I gripped both my forearms, but I couldn't actually feel the scars outside both jumper and jacket. They were there though, all over my arms, covering the skin that had once been smooth.

Once…

I couldn't actually remember a time when they had been. Likely I'd repressed it, along with a lot of other stuff that had happened to me. Maybe stuff that was worse than what I *did* remember, and that was horrible enough on its own.

But no thinking of Andrew!

If I fell into the darkness of what he had done, how he had ruined me, it would be a struggle to get myself back up. A struggle that mostly ended in the use of a razor. And I'd been harm-free for three months now—ever since I got out of my last hospitalisation. I wanted to keep it that way. I really did.

It didn't take me long to arrive at the café, and the bell jingled as I pushed the door open.

Mum was already there, sitting at a table with Harriet, the two of them bent close in a whispered conversation. They didn't look particularly happy. I hoped everything was okay between them. Mum had been happier the last three years, ever since I brought her to the café for the very first time so she could meet Damian. If it hadn't been for me, she never would've met Harriet.

The tingling of the bell drew Harriet's attention, as she was sitting facing the door and paid attention to her customers. And, I supposed anyway, she was working. She smiled slightly, but it was tight, and she rose and walked away before I even reached the table.

A ball of dread settled deep in my gut.

"What's that all about?" I stared after her. "I don't mind her joining us. I never have." If Harriet had a slow lunch hour, she always joined us for lunch. However, lunch tended to be the busiest time in the café—except not today. There were only a few other people in the room, besides us.

Did they have problems, Mum and Harriet? Just

the thought made my blood run cold. Mum had been so happy ever since they'd got together…

"I know, Joshua." Mum looked up at me and her expression was grim. It made me even more worried that something really *was* wrong. "I asked her to leave us alone. I need to talk to you."

I frowned as I sat down on the chair opposite her. "What's the matter? Is something wrong between you two? Are *you* all right?"

"I'm fine, Joshua, it's not me."

My frown deepened. "Is it Harriet? Or grandma? Or anyone else?"

Mum shook her head before fixing her eyes on me again. They were green, just like mine were. "It's about Andrew."

My blood really *did* run cold now, to the point I could feel it freeze in my veins. From the grim expression on her face, I knew whatever she had to say would not be good for my state of mind. "What is it?" I could hear how my voice shook. No one had ever scared me more than Andrew did, and the fear hadn't diminished much by the fact that I was now an adult and had been ever since they put him away. When the subject of Andrew came up, I still felt like the fifteen-year-old kid who didn't know how else to end the torment I was subjected to, other than killing myself.

Mum closed her eyes briefly. She seemed to struggle with what to say, but when her eyes opened again there was a determination in them. "He's been released on licence."

I swear my heart stopped beating. "But— He didn't confess! He was supposed to be incarcerated for all eight years." He hadn't been given any leniency, because he'd never admitted his wrongdoings.

Mum leaned over the table, taking my hands in hers and squeezing. "The system isn't fair—"

"It's bollocks!" My chest was tight. I didn't know if I wanted to rage or cry—probably both. "It's not *fair*."

"But Joshua, he's on licence. They keep track of him. He won't come near you ever again, I swear." She stared at me, hard, trying to make me understand her words.

I did understand them. But still… "What about when he's served his entire time? When they're not keeping an eye on him anymore? What's to stop him from seeking me out?" Just the thought of seeing Andrew again had me trembling from head to toe.

Mum frowned. "He's not going to risk going back to prison."

I wouldn't be so sure of that. "He wants revenge." No one knew Andrew better than me. For ten years I'd been his personal toy, to do with as he pleased. I knew just how vicious and sadistic he could be. My body still bore scars from his treatment, besides the ones I'd inflicted on myself. "Mum. I sent him to *prison*. He's punished me for a lot less than that." My eyes brimmed with tears as I tried to make her understand just what Andrew was capable of.

My last sentence got to her, I could tell from the way her frown fell away to be replaced by guilt. Guilt for never having noticed.

"Is he here in London?" London was big, but if Andrew was set on me, he'd find me. *Maybe he already had.* The dark shape on the street the night before flashed inside my mind.

"Joshua—" That was answer enough, her not wanting to confirm it, but I *needed* to hear it.

"Mum!"

"Yes." She closed her eyes. "Yes, he's here. But I don't know where. I only know he's out."

I pulled my hands out of her grip and put them in my lap, clenching and unclenching them. My body trembled, my mind whirled.

"Joshua…"

"I can't!" I stood so abruptly my chair toppled over. It didn't really matter though, not as long as my path to the door was clear.

"Don't do this, Joshua." Mum stood as well, her whole body tense. "Please. Calm down. Let's eat."

"No." I shook my head, eyes darting around. *Andrew's out. Out on the streets.* He was a sadistic, sociopathic abuser—and I was the one who'd put him in prison. "How could you let this happen?" I pressed my palm to my temples, emotions warring inside me.

"Joshua, please…"

I wasn't just afraid of Andrew—I was terrified. I wasn't sure if that was me being borderline or not, what with the disorder making me feel more intensely than normal people. Andrew had hurt me, beaten me, broken me, wounded me— And I'd been shattered all over again during the trial, having to see him sit there, without a single trace of remorse. Having to tell everything while he held steady that *I* was the liar.

I'd told nothing but the truth. He was the liar, unable to stand up to the things he'd done. He'd ruined my life… and he hadn't felt so much as a sliver of remorse for it. I'd felt his eyes on me, cold, hateful, full of rage, through the entire trial. I didn't believe for a second he'd continue with his life as if nothing had happened. He'd be back to hurt me again—I *knew* it!

"Joshua!"

Mum's voice called after me, but it was of no matter. I was out of there, running for my bloody *life*. How could the system let someone like him go? Didn't they realise he was going to do the very same thing he'd been sent to prison for again? Andrew thrived on the abuse, on the pain, on the power... he'd never give it up. If not me, he'd find someone else. Someone else who was unable to fight back, unable to get out of it, who didn't have anyone they could tell...

"Get down on your hands and knees. Brace your hands against the wall." His cold voice spoke from above me. He'd stripped me down until I was standing in front of him nude, and now he'd forcefully turned me around, so I was standing with my back to him.

Shivering, tears running freely, I did as he asked. It would end faster if I was silent and complied. It was what I lived by—it made my life just a tiny bit easier to just submit to him without a fight. Even if I hated myself afterwards.

I glanced over my shoulder and saw that Andrew was already rock hard. His jeans were undone, the flaps folded to each their side to show off the hard dick straining against the thin garment of his underpants. He had a sick glimpse in his eyes as he pulled his belt out of the loops. I knew perfectly well what he was going to do with it—something he'd done countless times before.

He ran his fingers over the black leather, almost lovingly. He caressed the buckle, licking his lips while he did so. Then he lifted his head to look me straight in the eye. "This is your own fault, Joshua. Remember that."

I turned back to the wall with a choked sob. I squeezed my eyes shut as I bit down on my lower lip, so hard I wouldn't make a single sound when the whipping started. So hard it drew blood. But drawing blood was better than giving him the satisfaction of making me scream.

But once the leather, once the buckle, whipped over my back with all the force he possessed— all my pretence of not making a sound was forgotten as all-consuming pain shot through me.

CHAPTER 2

*I*t was dark outside when I finally ventured home. I'd been walking aimlessly around central London, trying to sort myself out. It hadn't worked. All I could think of was Andrew, what he'd done to me, and what he *would* do to me once he got to me.

I didn't know the time. I'd turned my phone off once I'd stopped running, because I didn't want Mum to keep ringing me.

Three years... It had only been three years. How could they have let him out already? He was a danger to any kid he got a hold of. He shouldn't ever have been let out on the streets again! Didn't anyone realise...?

The streets were all but deserted. I didn't meet

many people once I neared home. The sound of my trainers was the only thing I could hear—the only thing that existed—as I continued along the pavement. The cars that passed didn't even draw my attention. They weren't important.

What was important was that the legal system had let a dangerous person out on the streets, where he could target and hurt whoever he liked. And me—he would definitely hurt me. I wasn't a child anymore, but he'd been obsessed... he was a paedophile, but if that obsession was still intact, it likely wouldn't matter that I was an adult now.

The hairs on the back of my neck stood up. My whole body tensed. Someone was behind me. I couldn't hear anything but traffic and my own trainers hitting the pavement, but I knew it with a ringing certainty.

I dared a quick look over my shoulder. No one there.

I faced forwards again. Two people were coming towards me on the opposite side of the road, but they were young. Their voices started to carry as they came closer: a bloke and a girl. Nothing to worry about. But the hairs at the back of my neck were still on full alert.

Someone *was* behind me, and that someone was watching me.

I quickened my pace. It wasn't long before I reached our building, and my hands shook as I fished my keys out of my pocket and stuck the right one in the lock. A click and it was open, and I all but ripped the key back out before slipping inside and closing the door hard behind me. A flick of my wrist and it was locked again.

No one could follow me inside now.

I ran over to our door, unlocked that one, and slipped inside again, only opening it as much as needed to fit me in-between it and the wall. I locked this door safely after me too, then collapsed on the floor in a heap. My breathing was laboured after the running—but it was nothing compared to the pain. The pain of the memories. The pain of Andrew. The pain of remembering. The pain of *knowing*. Of knowing he was out there, that he was free, once again. Free to do as he wished, free to ruin more lives.

That's what he did. He ruined lives. There was nothing at all good about him. He was evil, sadistic, a psychopath who thrived on inflicting pain. Who thrived on humiliation and power and violence.

I wrapped my arms over my head, whimpering into the carpet.

If I'd never put him in prison, he never would've had cause for revenge. But if I *hadn't* put him in prison, he would've continued doing whatever he wanted with me. For longer than the ten years he'd managed to do so undetected. Or maybe I'd have succeeded in killing myself on my second try, because I didn't doubt for a second I would've tried again if I hadn't come clean to Mum—if she hadn't believed me.

I would've tried again and again and again—until I succeeded. Because I hadn't been able to take it anymore. Not any of it. I'd been used as his punching bag and pleasure slave for as long as I could remember.

How could they let someone like that go free? He'd started molesting me when I was a *child*. I couldn't remember a time when he *hadn't* used me for his own pleasure. When I wasn't deathly afraid of nights, because that was usually when he came into my room. In the beginning, anyway.

I pushed up on my hands and knees and crawled to the end of the carpet, then used the wall to help me up into a standing position. My emotions weighed me down so much I had trouble keeping myself on my feet.

I wanted to scream, to cut myself up—but none of it would make it better. None of it would put Andrew back in prison, where he belonged. None of it would make proper justice be served.

"Damian…" He was asleep. He must be, because the flat was as dark as it was outside and all was silent.

I stumbled into our bedroom, hoping he was asleep, because if he wasn't there it wouldn't end well for me and my skin. But he was. Sleeping peacefully, that is.

Guilt washed over me as my knees hit the mattress, but it didn't stop me from reaching out and shaking him. "Damian. *Damian*."

He groaned, slapping at my hand. "What?"

"Damian, please. I need you."

He stilled for a second, then rolled over onto his back so he could peer up at me. "You're home."

I sniffled and crawled up fully on the bed, curling up next to him. "I need you. I just need you."

"Hey." He sat up, embracing me. I fell into his arms and buried my face against his neck and shoulder. "I'm always here for you, you know that."

I clutched him close, but it wasn't enough. We weren't close enough, so I moved to straddle his thighs, arms locking tight around his neck as I once again buried my face in the crook of it. "I'm sorry I woke you. I just need you so badly." To think that this morning I'd woken up feeling *good*, and now I was anything but.

"I don't mind, Josh. It's better than you resorting

to cutting." He rested his cheeks against my hair. "I'm so proud of you for being harm-free for three months, you know."

Proud... "I know you are." I whispered it, breath fanning over his sleep-warm skin. I knew very well he was proud of me for not resorting to cutting for so long. "You should go back to sleep. You've got school in the morning." I said it, I meant it, but I couldn't let him go.

"I was waiting up for you." Now he sounded guilty. And come to think of it... He seemed to be wearing proper clothes instead of the soft, casual ones he used to sleep in. "But obviously I fell asleep."

"Why'd you wait up for me?" Then I remembered. We'd been supposed to spend some quality time together, without our flatmates around. "I'm sorry. I forgot. I'm so sorry." His guilt was nothing compared to mine. It consumed me.

"Josh..." His arms tightened around me. "You honestly think I wouldn't wait up? Your mum rang me, you know. She didn't reach me before tonight, once I got home and turned the ringer on on my phone. All day you've known, and I didn't find out until only hours ago."

Of course Mum would've rung him when I never answered. And of course he kept his phone on silent at school. He was busy, he had a lot of studying, and he couldn't let his phone disrupt him. Not when I'd been in a good mood in the morning. There was no harm to be done then, to keep his phone on silent and not check it. Only, harm had already been done...

"Do you want to lie down?"

I nodded jerkily and he gently pushed me down on the bed. When I was lying on my side, with my back to him, he scooted in close and wrapped an arm tightly around my waist.

"It'll get better, Josh. Just give it time." He kissed the back of my neck, making me shudder. No matter how bad I was feeling, having him so close, being so intimate, it was *good*. "He won't get to you."

I drew in a shaky breath, but didn't say anything. He didn't know. How could he possibly know it would get better? I'd been getting better the past three months only, but I always seemed to revert. And now... now it was impossible. Now Andrew was out there, possibly—no, definitely—out for revenge.

He must want it. He couldn't have changed so much the past three years. Well, the past five, considering he'd been kept out of my life ever since I woke up in hospital and told Mum. The man I knew, the sadistic pervert who'd ruined me, he'd do anything he could to punish me for what I'd done. Prison couldn't have changed him for the better. I whole-heartedly believed he couldn't ever change. He'd always been out to hurt me—and he would *still* be out to hurt me.

I turned around in Damian's arms, pressing up close to him. "I love you so much."

"I love you too."

I should tell him. About my feelings, just how intense they were. About Andrew and my absolute certainty that he was out for me. About the dark shape outside the window last night—*oh god!*—and someone following me home now, except I hadn't actually seen anyone.

But he had enough on his mind. He was in medical school, studying to become a surgeon, and he had enough on his mind. Besides, I was twenty-one years old. I should be able to take care of myself by now.

Except I was exceptionally bad at just that.

"*N*o—st-stop, no!"

I was pressed down into the bed and hands were grabbing me forcefully. My body ached from the rough treatment. I was hurting, I was being hurt, it hurt so bloody much! I was always hurting, it kept happening again and again and again… and I didn't want it to happen, I wanted him off me, I didn't want to lie there naked in my own bed with him atop me, forcing me…

"No! Ge-get off me!"

I tried to push him off, but he was too heavy and I was too weak. I was too weak to do anything but lie there and take every hurtful touch. I had to lie there and take the harsh words, the slapping, the beating, the grunting when he forced himself on me.

Panic shot through me as my legs were shoved apart and he forced his way down in-between them.

"No!" I screamed, only to have a big, rough hand come up to cover my mouth. The hand was so huge it was covering my nose as well and I couldn't breathe. I flailed my arms, which he'd let go of in order to cover my mouth. I hit something, someone, but he didn't move away from me. Instead he pressed down further and I wanted to scream again, but I couldn't because that hand was shutting off my airways and I couldn't breathe...

"o!"

I shot up into a sitting position. The duvet tangled around my feet and my clothes clung to my damp skin. My heart beat wildly and my breathing was ragged. I bent over, hands buried in my hair as I fought the tears and the sobs. I pulled violently on my hair, hoping the pain would hold the tears in check.

"Damian...?"

The bed next to me was empty and reality slowly sank back in. Damian was already at school. I'd slept in, slept longer than I used to. Usually, if I didn't wake up long before him, I woke up alongside him. But I'd slept in, which meant he wasn't there. He wasn't there to wake me from the nightmare, he wasn't there to hold and calm me down…

My breathing sped up again and I crawled to the end of the bed. Even though my body was drenched in sweat from the fear the nightmare had brought back, the chill in the room was creeping in on me. I stumbled onto the floor and stood there for a while, lost as to what to do next, before I fled to the bathroom. Unlike the bedroom, it was warm and I didn't even bother turning on the lights as I sank down on the heated floor, lying atop the soft, fluffy rug.

I curled one hand in front of my face and, though I couldn't see it, knew exactly how it looked: deformed by scars. Without realising it, my other hand had started scratching at my scarred skin. Quickly, I pulled it back and started rapidly snapping the rubber bands I always wore around each wrist now. I hadn't cut myself in three months. I couldn't slip up now, not after so long without it. How could I face anyone if I slipped up again? How could I face *Damian*? *Proud*…

The images from the nightmare flashed in my mind. I covered my face with my hands and forced down the shriek that threatened to leave me.

My arms were itching. I wanted a razor, I wanted to cut, I *needed* to cut. After all these years, I was still plagued by the nightmares. It was five years ago now that I'd tried to kill myself and Andrew's abuse had finally ended. Five years and it was still ruining my life.

He was still ruining my life.

And now he was out.

Why couldn't the nightmares ever stop? Why couldn't I ever be free from Andrew and the abuse I'd suffered at his hands for almost my entire childhood? Why couldn't I ever get over it so I could live a nice, normal life? Why did I have to be so continuously messed up? Whenever I thought things were finally going well, when I'd gone three months without cutting, the nightmares returned full force to slap me right across the face. And now his release hit me like a sledgehammer.

The tears were falling now and I didn't even bother wiping them away. There was no point; they were going to fall anyway. Instead I clenched my hands in against my chest. I had to resist the temptation to search the entire bathroom for a razor or to scratch myself until I bled, something I had resorted to so many times in the past I couldn't even count anymore.

Blood calmed me down like nothing else did. Seeing it trickle over my scars, struggling to find a path through the deformed, scarred skin... it was fascinating, it was addicting, it was something I'd needed for so very long. Something I *still* needed.

I was shaking from anxiety and restraint and tears were constantly pressing behind my eyelids. I was sweating too, and it was a cold sweat that left me feeling chilly all over. I was hanging on by a thread. Now there were only a couple of thin, frail threads left and I was slowly losing the battle. I couldn't hang onto them.

Why should I?

I was alive today because cutting had helped me deal. If it hadn't been for that... I doubted I'd be alive and breathing and *panicking* today.

I pushed myself up as the tears overflowed, trailing down my cheeks. I all but ran to the kitchen, grabbed the first knife I could find, then darted back into the bathroom again. I locked the door after me, even though I was the only one at home. Or so I hoped anyway. Damian was gone for school the entire day, and both Silver and Kian had jobs to go to.

The wood was hard against my back as I leant against it, trying to will myself to leave the bathroom again, but I couldn't. Couldn't possibly leave. I needed... needed release. Needed it so badly I trembled with it.

When I managed to get the trembling slightly under control, I stumbled over to the bathtub and climbed inside. It was safe in there, small enough to fit me lying down, and the sides shielded everything else from view.

I pulled my jumper over my head, leaving me in a T-shirt. I put the knife down in front of me, close to the drain. It was sharp. It was just what I needed. Just what I craved. Just what could give me that blessed release.

Andrew. Andrew… He shouldn't be allowed to be *out*. He was dangerous. Didn't they realise that?

I squeezed my eyes shut as a sob escaped me, and I pressed the blade of the knife down into my scarred and mutilated skin, drawing blood for the first time in three months. I'd never been able to go three months without cutting before.

Andrew's eyes… whenever they'd met mine during the court case… they'd been so cold. Promising revenge. London might be big, but if Andrew wanted to get back at me for his incarceration, then he bloody well could. How could I know he hadn't found me already? He might be watching me, might've been following me. Because someone *had* been watching, and someone *had* followed me.

What if he knew where I lived? I was so sure the person outside had been looking in our window.

What if he came knocking on the door when I was home alone? Nothing would stop him from breaking it down and having his way with me. Nothing at all. I might be a grown up now, but if I was faced with him… I'd be just as powerless to defend myself as I had been when I'd been a kid.

Someone was out there watching last night. Someone followed me tonight.

Fear laced through me.

Opening my eyes, I stared down at my left arm. The blood was trickling already. Some stained my jeans, some dripped into the tub itself. The stark red colour next to the white of the tub… such a contrast. Such beauty.

They let him out. I can't believe they let him out. I cut again, and again, and again. I cut until my entire forearm was covered in red. My jeans were completely ruined; the tub was dotted red—more red than it was white by now.

Tears ran in a steady stream down my cheeks and sobs wracked my body. My right hand was shaking and covered in the blood it had drawn. The knife was slippery in my fingers, but I couldn't stop cutting. It had been so long since the last time…

"*I'm so proud of you.*" Damian's words echoed through my mind. *Damian!* The knife clattered to the bottom of the tub as I curled in on myself. I went to cover my face with my hands, but then realised they were covered in blood, so I settled on burying my face against the scarred skin on my right arm, which I hadn't cut yet.

One piece of bad news and I was back to being a mess. I wasn't doing any better at all. I was the very same mess I'd been my entire bloody *life*. Since Andrew had literally fucked me up. *"Proud of you…"* How could Damian even stand to look at me now? I'd slipped up after three months and for what? For Andrew. Like I always did. Everything was *always* about Andrew. He kept on messing up my life when he wasn't even part of it anymore.

I tried to stop the blood with my right hand, but it kept on trickling. I'd cut too much, too deep, and no matter how hard I pressed, I couldn't stop it.

"Oh god, no. No, no, no, *no*."

I'd lost control.

I fished out my phone from my other pocket—I'd fallen asleep with it, and in my clothes—, and I unlocked the screen to stare at the names on my recently-called list. Damian was on top. I could ring him, but he was at school so not likely to hear it unless he checked it at that exact moment. I could ring Mum, and she'd drop everything for me, like she always did. Guilt gnawed at me. How long was I going to keep inconveniencing everyone close to me?

I clicked on the second option.

"Joshua?"

"Mum," I cried into the phone. "I cut myself again."

"Wha—" She sounded confused for a moment. "Joshua, what happened? What's the matter?"

"*I cut myself!*" I bent over, placing my phone against my ear and shoulder as I tried to press down on my arm again. It didn't do any good. I couldn't reach all the cuts—they were all over. "Mum, I cut too deep."

She drew a sharp breath. "Keep pressure on it. I'll be right there." Only a click alerted me to the fact she'd hung up.

I rested my forehead against my knees, crying loudly. The pain from the cutting helped calm my emotions a bit, but not nearly enough. Everything was still so overwhelming, and on a constant loop in my mind.

I rocked back and forth as I cried and the blood kept trickling from my arm, messing up the tub, me, everything. Maybe I'd just bleed out in there and that would be that.

No! I couldn't do that to Damian. Not to Mum either. I couldn't *die*. I had so many people I cared about, people I didn't want to leave. Living *hurt*, but at least I had them close to me. My family, Damian's family, my friends…

I must've been like that for a long time, because

next thing I knew someone was banging on the front door. Keys rattled, door was opened then closed. More banging on the bathroom door.

"Joshua! Open up."

It took me way too long to push myself up and stumble over to the door, but I managed it. I turned the lock so she'd be able to come inside, then collapsed down on the fluffy rug in a fit of hysterics.

"Joshua!" Her hands cupped my face, tilting it up so I faced her. She swam in front of my eyes, in and out of focus. "Jesus. What have you done?"

"I'm sorry!" I crumbled again into fits of sobs.

"No, I'm sorry. I didn't mean it like that. I'm not blaming you." Her hands left my face and she walked away, but she was soon back with a wet towel she pressed against my bleeding arm. "You need sutures. We have to go to A&E."

A jerky nod was all I could manage in response. I knew I'd cut too deep, I knew wrapping it up wouldn't stop the bleeding.

She cleaned what she could, though new blood kept trickling, so it was impossible to get it all off. Once she was satisfied—or frustrated enough—she wrapped gauze tightly around my arm so it would hopefully hold until we got me to the A&E, where they'd stitch me up.

"Up you go then." She wasn't as tall as me, except

when she was wearing heels, but she was still strong, and she managed to pull me up on my feet without much help from me.

I wanted to thank her, but my throat wouldn't produce sound. My tongue was stuck to the roof of my mouth. I was terrified, humiliated, and ashamed. I'd slipped up so badly I had to get sutures—it had been *months* since the last time I'd had to go to A&E for that. Four months now—and that time had ended me up back in hospital for a month.

And once again, it was Mum helping me. Like she always did.

J heard mum's heels click against the linoleum floor, and I glanced around the corner to check if she was alone. She was—and she was pacing, eyes locked on a document she held in her hands.

"Mum?" I shuffled into view, the sleeves of my jumper drawn down so much the hem was bunched in my palms. I hunched over, nervous and afraid.

"Yes?" She kept on pacing, kept on reading that document. Whatever it was.

"Isn't Andrew home?"

"He left for a business meeting this morning. He'll be gone a couple days." Back and forth over the floor, eyes glued to the paper.

"Mum…" My body ached from the night before,

it bore the evidence of his perversions. If she'd just look at me, she'd see my lip bore it as well.

"I don't have time right now, Joshua. I have to prepare for this."

It was like a black hole appeared under me and sucked me in. *She doesn't have time… No time for me.* "I'm sorry. I won't bother you."

She made a sound, but I wasn't sure what it was supposed to represent. Maybe relief at me leaving her alone to do whatever she needed to do for work.

"I'm sorry."

"I'll see you tonight." She brushed past me, not even so much as glancing my way.

It was like I was standing there with a gaping hole in my gut, spilling blood and intestines all over the floor. She wasn't interested in listening to me, to hearing what I had to say. She couldn't even look at me.

How could I ever expect her to believe me when she wouldn't ever give me the time of day? Not a hug, not a squeeze on the shoulder, not a *look*— She didn't care what Andrew was doing to me, what he'd done for so long. Maybe she knew? Maybe she'd always known… She didn't care about me.

I was nothing to her.

I'd tried approaching her and been dismissed. Because her work was more important than me. I was nothing to her, nothing to anyone, except for Andrew—

Who used me for his own pleasure.

That was all I was—all I ever would be. I'd never get away. Not when even my own mum couldn't give me the time of day so I could tell her. If she did give me the time of day, I doubted she'd even believe me.

Best to keep it hidden, deep down, like I had for so long. Best not let her know. Best to just let Andrew have his way, so it'd be simpler for me. Best to just give in.

Because I was nothing.

I had no one.

CHAPTER 4

*S*itting in an exam room waiting for a doctor to deign to come in wasn't a good feeling. I was cried out, ashamed, and being left to wait for someone to have the time to deal with me humiliating. My arm burned from my own treatment earlier, but that pain was nothing to the humiliation I felt at having slipped up so badly.

Being stitched up was almost a relief, because it brought more pain, but the pain I'd inflicted on myself was being repaired. Well, not repaired, but at least sown back together so I wouldn't bleed out.

Mum, who'd had to wait outside while they fixed me up, jumped up from her chair the moment she saw me coming. "How are you?" She stared anxiously at my arm, where the new bandage was covered by my jumper.

"Stitched up." That wasn't what she wanted to hear, likely, but I couldn't lie to her either. I couldn't say I was good when I was anything but.

"Come on, Joshua. Let's get you home. You need rest. And you need to change clothes."

She was right about that. My arm and hair wasn't the only ting covered in blood. I probably looked like I'd come right from a massacre. And I had, hadn't I? A massacre of my own skin.

I trailed after her outside, cradling my stitched-up arm close to my chest.

We didn't speak as she drove towards home. I sat with my head resting against the cool glass, and she was busy steering the roads in the rain. I hadn't even noticed the rain until now.

When we got back to the flat, Mum came inside with me without a word. I was secretly grateful, because I didn't trust myself on my own. Not now. Not with me a mess—and with the bathroom still a mess. If I'd been alone, I could've very well gone back in there and done the same to my right arm as I'd done to my left.

"Oh my god, the *bathroom*."

Mum looked at me, at my horrified realisation. "I'll clean it. Don't worry."

I nodded jerkily, grateful she volunteered for the task.

"Come on. You need to get changed." She wrapped an arm around my shoulder and steered me towards my bedroom. "I'll clean the bathroom while you do that. Don't worry."

It didn't take me long to change into joggers and one of Damian's big, comfy jumpers. One of those with a hood. He wasn't all that fond of them, except using them at home, but I loved burying myself in them. I loved that they were too big on me, that they seemed to swallow me. They were his and they were a comfort whenever he wasn't around. They were when he was home too though, but they could never be as much of a comfort to me as being close to Damian was.

I went over to collapse on the sofa, curling in on myself.

Mum came out of the bathroom with the knife, disappearing into the kitchen with it. I heard the sink run, heard her wash it, then silence for a minute before she came back to sink down next to me.

"In all honesty, Joshua, I feel like I never should've told you."

My blood ran cold. "Of course you should have." It came out with conviction. "I'd rather know and be a mess, than to have to suddenly see him or have him appear in front of me. At least now I *know* he's out there." I *knew* who was stalking me.

"He won't come near you, Joshua. You hear that? If he so much as looks in your direction, I'll have him hauled off to prison again."

"But Mum— Even if he doesn't come after me— he'll still hurt someone else. Three years in prison won't change the fact that he's a sadistic tosser who gets off on *kids*." I was shaking, trembling from head to foot.

"He's only on licence. They're keeping an eye on him. If he does hurt someone else, he'll be locked up again. For a lot longer this time." Mum sighed again. "Sadly, there's not much *I* can do about preventing him from hurting anyone, Joshua."

"It's not fair." No one should have to go through what I'd gone through.

"Nothing ever is." Mum had a far-away look on her face, then she shook it off. "Are you hungry? I'll order us some takeout."

I nodded quickly, though my stomach was likely too knotted up with pain and worry and bad memories to eat anything. Mum rose to make the call. I didn't know what she planned on ordering and I didn't really care.

My eyes went to the windows. The curtains weren't drawn, which meant Damian must've parted them before he headed off to school. I'd certainly not touched them since last night.

It was light out, though it felt like it should be dark. It felt like the whole day had gone by, but it had only been a few hours. I squinted at the windows. I couldn't see anyone though, not like last night. Couldn't see a shape out there, looking right into our living room. Couldn't see a person look in, though a lot of them walked past. Maybe I hadn't really seen something the night before, either. Maybe it was just a figment of my imagination. Maybe I'd simply been tired. There were a lot of explanations—better ones than *Andrew's stalking me.*

Surely it couldn't be him.

But the fact that Mum was here… that made me feel a lot better. Because no matter what I tried to tell myself, I wasn't at all sure. I was sure I'd seen someone the night before last—and my gut told me it *had* been Andrew. But who would believe me if I told them?

Everyone was convinced he wasn't going to risk more prison time by coming near me again.

They didn't know him. Damian had never met him, and Mum didn't know him either. He'd put on an act all those years for her. I was the only one who knew what a monster he was.

And I knew I wasn't safe. I knew he was out there, biding his time. That he'd want revenge.

SIX YEARS AGO

I groaned in pain as I was shoved forcefully to the floor, my knees taking the brunt of it before I fell face-first. I quickly turned over so I could stare up at Andrew, terror coursing through me. When he started out violent, it always escalated.

"Joshua," he drawled lazily, gazing down at me with lust. His lust was evident in other places of his anatomy too.

I trembled as he grabbed me, pulling me back up on my feet. I tried stepping back, away from him, but he kept a tight hold of my upper arms. I'd have bruises there tomorrow to join all the others I already had.

He started ripping off my clothes, and that's

when my tears began falling. I stood quietly, though, as he undressed me. It was always over quicker if I didn't fight against him, if I didn't fight back, and that was the only good thing about it. Even if I hated myself after.

When he finished ridding me of my clothes, he shoved me down on my bed face-first. I heard him fumble with his clothes, then he grabbed me again, lifting me up and positioning me so I was on my hands and knees.

"Good boy," he murmured as he lined up behind me. "You're such a good boy, Joshua. Now, be just as good while taking it. I know you love it. This is what you were born for."

My head dropped to the mattress as I did my best to stifle my sobs. I didn't love this, I wasn't born for it… I hated it! I hated him. I hated him so much.

I wish he died. Or I died. Whichever, I wasn't picky. As long as I didn't have to take this anymore—

CHAPTER 5

The shame of sitting in A&E, wounded, bloody and waiting to be stitched up, was nothing compared to the shame I felt once Damian came home. He was early, a lot earlier than usual, home before both Silver and Kian, which was quite unusual these days.

I bent my head down, not able to face him. "I'm sorry. I'm so sorry." I tried to fight the pressing tears, I really did.

"What are you sorry for?" I could hear he was bewildered. Of course he was. He had no idea.

"Josh…"

Mum moved away from me, and Damian took her seat. I still couldn't look at him.

His hand gently touched my arm, just barely brushing the fabric of the jumper.

"Why'd you cut again, Josh? Three months…"

"I know it's been three months!" I hadn't planned on yelling at him, but it erupted from me like lava from a volcano. "I know I *failed*. Like I fail everything!"

"Josh, I never said—" We were so close his knee and thigh rested against mine.

"He's out," I whispered, anguished. "He's out on the streets."

"Josh…"

Sobs overcame me, big ones that hurt and took my breath away. "I'm *so* sorry."

He tipped me sideways so I could rest my head on his shoulder. "You've got nothing to be sorry for." He whispered it close to my ear. "I know better than anyone what his actions are still doing to you."

He *should* know, yeah, considering he shared a bed with me. He woke me up from the nightmares whenever they were particularly bad—except when he wasn't *there*. *I hate late mornings*. Every morning he wasn't there in the bed with me, was the worst morning in my entire existence.

"If he gets hold of me, he'll hurt me again. And if not, he'll hurt someone else. No matter what, I can't even bear to think about it." I sniffled, curling my arms up against my chest, feeling the sting of pain as I pressed them close. "I couldn't take it, so I cut. I cut deep."

His arms around me tightened, a tell-tale sign he was distressed. "How much? How much did you cut?"

"Over all of it." All the old scars. "On my left arm." At least my right one was unscathed—or as unscathed as it could be, being completely covered in old scars.

"Did he see anyone at the hospital?" This question was directed at Mum.

She didn't answer verbally, so I assumed she shook her head.

"If I'm going to see anyone, it's Vincent." I didn't want to speak to anyone else. He'd been with me ever since my suicide attempt, five years ago now. He knew everything about me.

"I'm so sorry." I couldn't stop saying it. I'd failed *again*. When would I ever *stop* failing at every single thing in my life?

"Josh." He squeezed my shoulder, hugging me tightly. "You don't have to apologise to me. Not for anything, not ever."

Of course I did. I messed up—he had to deal with it… of course I had to apologise. Once again I'd let

Andrew drag me back down into despair, even after all these years…

"You've got blood in your hair." He touched said hair, then broke the hug and stood up. I heard him walk away.

I hunched on the sofa, listening anxiously to what he was doing. Was he leaving me? But no… He came back with a wet cloth. The water was warm, he'd made sure it wouldn't be cold, as he washed the blood out of my hair. I hoped he got everything—I didn't relish sitting there with blood all over me. Though I *had* walked into A&E with blood all over me, clothes and all, so what did it really matter if I sat like this at home?

The front door opened, and both Silver and Kian spilled inside, joking and laughing with each other. They were so easy-going with each other. Damian and I had never had that. I had issues too big to ever be so carefree.

Their smiles faded simultaneously as they got a good look at me, and the cloth Damian was using to wash the blood out of my hair.

I looked away. I couldn't face seeing more disappointment.

"Hey, lads." It was Mum greeting them. I was too busy staring at the black telly. I didn't know what else Damian was doing, besides scrubbing my head with the wet cloth.

"What's happened?" Silver. He sounded worried. Well, he should be. He'd been living with me for three years, he knew how it usually ended. Hospitalised, until I got better. Then a period of all being well, before the downward spiral started again. Same bloody pattern every bloody time. It never stopped.

"I'll tell you later," Damian said and I supposed he must be silently communicating with Silver. They'd been mates a long time—they knew each other well. And Silver didn't say anything else, because he understood.

"You can just tell them. I'm going to take a shower." I felt dirty. Shamed and humiliated.

Mum grabbed my unharmed arm as I stood up. "Careful of the stitches."

"Yeah, I know. I've done this before, you know." I whispered it, it wasn't an accusation or anything like that, but she drew in a sharp breath anyway. *Go me.* Reminding her yet again what a mess I was—what *he'd* made me.

The bathroom was warm and empty and any traces of blood was gone. I didn't know if it was heaven or hell. Maybe both. When I was with people, I wanted to be alone. When I was alone, I wanted to be with someone. The bathroom was the most triggering room in the flat. *This is where I always ended up, curled on the floor or in the bathtub, arm cut up, blood all over…*

I kept my injured arm braced against the wall as I showered. The shower head faced away from it, the hot water hitting me anywhere *but* that arm. The gauze was relatively dry when I got out, only a few damp spots.

I dressed in the clothes I'd only changed into a few hours before. Comfort clothes, though they weren't of much comfort now. Maybe Damian would be, especially if we were alone.

They were all there when I came out. Talking about me, which was obvious from the way they stopped talking once the bathroom door opened. What had they been saying about me?

"I'm going to bed." I couldn't face them anyway. I wanted to be alone, after all.

Silver's attention moved away from me, instead he focused on Kian. He made a motion with his head towards the kitchen, and Kian nodded briefly.

"I'm sorry, Josh." Silver's grey eyes met mine.

I looked down, unable to make eye-contact. Gave a tiny nod.

"I'm sorry." That was Kian, his voice lighter, more high-pitched than Silver's deep one.

A tiny nod again. Still staring at the floor.

They headed into the kitchen, leaving me with just Damian and Mum to face. I was grateful to Mum for all she'd done, for coming to me no matter what she'd been in the middle of, and for staying with me. But right now all I wanted was Damian all to myself.

Mum must've sensed it. Or read it on my face or in my body language or whatever.

"You're in good hands now. I'll leave the two of you alone." She came over and hugged me, something she only did when things were really bad. She wasn't much of a hugger, never had been, but after finding out about Andrew she tried her best. Like I did. We both tried our best in a shitty situation.

"Thank you." *For everything*.

"There's nothing to thank me for. I'll always be here for you."

Was she ever going to stop being guilty for never noticing? That was probably as likely as me forgetting what had happened to me. We'd both have to live with it for the rest of our lives. Be messed up about it.

She left. Now there was only Damian, and I finally dared lift my head. He was studying me, all silent and thoughtful.

"Say something." I couldn't stand silence. Not now. Not when I'd messed up and I didn't know what would happen next. Would this be the time he'd had enough?

"I wish you'd rung me."

More guilt. "You were at school."

"I had my phone on." He came closer, put his hands on my shoulder. "Andrew's been released from jail... You really think I'd keep my phone off right now? I know how much the thought of him still haunts you. I wanted to be available in case you needed something."

"I didn't know." I bent my head again. "You didn't say."

He drew me into an embrace. "I didn't think I had to."

I lifted my arms slowly, almost hesitantly, and then I was clinging onto him for dear life. Like he was the only thing that could keep me grounded, that could keep me in the here and now, and not fall further into that endlessly black spiral.

"You want to go to bed?" He said it against my ear, his cheek resting against mine.

"You've just come home. You haven't eaten or anything."

"Doesn't matter." He steered us in the direction of the bedroom. "Come on."

I was too weak to argue with him about it. Too

selfish, because all I did want was to have him in bed with me.

He changed into his comfy clothes when we got into the bedroom while I sank down on the bed, watching him. He really had a nice body, all tall and lanky and toned. It was too bad I never got to see it much. The both of us always slept in clothes, and it wasn't like we ever did anything intimate that required the loss of them.

"What?"

He'd caught me looking. "Nothing."

"You were thinking hard about something." He came over to stand in front of me.

I looked up. "Just admiring the view."

His eyes narrowed a fraction. I didn't know if he either didn't understand my meaning or if he didn't appreciate it. I'd said it to him before, we'd been together three years after all, but he always seemed to wriggle out of the topic, changing it.

He bent over, hands grabbing both sides of my face, and then he kissed me.

If anything could get my mind onto something else, it was kissing him. It was something that didn't happen all that often. I knew he loved me, but he wasn't interested in intimacy. Not sex, which he was completely uninterested in. He didn't *dislike* kissing though, but I definitely cared more for it than him.

What I definitely didn't care for was him standing while I was sitting. I wanted him on the bed with me, so I leaned backwards, and he followed without breaking the kiss.

He landed on me, and considering everything that had happened to me during my childhood, the feel of another man atop of me should've made me panic. It didn't, not with him. I *wanted* him, but he didn't want me, not in quite the way I craved him.

I knew it, and he knew it, and we managed. I had no desire to have sex with anyone else though, so I managed with my right hand. Or left, whichever worked at the time. That didn't happen often either though, mostly in my good periods. And they didn't come around often and sure didn't stay that way for a long time.

Besides, sex had never given me anything good in my life. Especially not with Andrew, but never really with the one-offs I'd indulged in either. But life with Damian, without sex, was as good as I would likely ever feel.

He broke the kiss and rolled over, so now we were both on our backs, shoulder to shoulder.

"Will you ring me next time?"

"Next time I need to go to A&E?"

"Well, yeah, but I meant generally. Whenever you need to." He grabbed my hand, twining our fingers together. "I'll always be here for you, no matter what else I've got to do. You and your health come first."

That was sweet of him. I rolled over, rested my head on his shoulder and put my stitched-up hand on his chest. He had a scar hidden underneath that T-shirt, a big one going from shoulder to hip. It was part of why he never showed much skin around me —and especially not around anyone else.

"I will." Unless I wouldn't. I was aware of how I could be, about what came with my disorder. Unstable emotions, impulsiveness... plus a whole host of other things, but those were the big ones with me. Oh, and the self-injury part too.

"Good." His arm curled over my back, hand gripping my shoulder.

I drew in a deep breath, slowly let it out. Laying like this was good. Me and him, together. Nothing could hurt me here in bed, with only the two of us. Nothing but nightmares, anyway, there was no stopping them.

FIVE YEARS AGO

"*H*i, Joshua." The cold voice came from behind me, the goose bumps flashing down my spine as all thoughts disappeared from my mind. Strong hands grabbed me, pulled me further into the house.

I stumbled and crashed to the floor as he shoved me through my bedroom door. I tried to catch myself with my hands, but my wrists gave out and the meeting with the cold floor was painful.

Andrew stepped inside after me and as I heard the door close, I knew this was it. There was no getting away from him. Not that I ever could, but I always hoped I would, anyway.

I lay still on the floor, my eyes squeezed shut and arms folded underneath my chest. He sighed in annoyance, then reached down, grabbing the back of my shirt and yanking me back up.

He slammed me up against the wall, and I couldn't help the pained grunt that left me. His free hand came up, closing around my neck, tightening dangerously. He smirked at me as my eyes flew open, the tears welling involuntarily as I struggled to breathe.

"Tell me, Joshua." He was snarling now. "Where've you been all night? I've been waiting for you. You never showed up."

His grip loosened enough for me to answer. "Didn't know I had a curfew." It came out strangled, hoarse, and then I gasped again as his grip tightened back up. This would leave a bruise—if it didn't leave me dead of asphyxiation first.

"Don't be smart with me!"

"Let me go!" I clawed at his forearm in a vain attempt to try and fight myself free. I was losing my breath fast, he was clutching my throat so tight—

"Tell me where you've been!" He loosened his grip again.

"Partying! I've been out partying!"

"Is that the truth?" He asked it in a low, dangerous tone. "Just partying?"

"Yes! It's the truth!" It wasn't. Not by a long shot.

But if I hurled it in his face now I'd gone and had sex with someone else, he'd kill me for sure.

"I don't know if I believe you." His grip tightened again. "I don't believe you at all, you little twat." With that, he stepped away, hand falling away from my throat.

I ducked forward into a severe coughing fit, and now it was my hands at my neck, touching the skin lightly, feeling the damage.

"Good little liar you've become, hmm?" He came back up close to me, hands pulling at my clothes.

The tears fell then, running freely down my cheeks as I realised I wasn't going to get away. That he wasn't going to back off. But I didn't fight; I never fought it, because I just wanted it to end. The more pliant I was, the quicker he was out of my bed and back in his own.

But it only served to make me hate myself more.

CHAPTER 6

"*J*osh?"

"No!" I groaned, rolling away from the shaking. "No, please!" Not again, I couldn't take another round.

"Josh!"

A warm hand cupped my cheek, stroking lovingly. *He never does that.*

"Josh, come on. Wake up."

The voice was close to my ear and then a cheek rested against mine. There was light stubble on it, and it was all very familiar. "*Damian.*" I reached up, tangling my fingers in his hair, holding him down tight against me.

"Yeah. You're okay now. You were only dreaming." His arms slid around me.

I drew a shaky breath. My throat felt raw, hurting, like I truly had just been choked. I wondered if I got up right now to look at myself in the mirror, if there would be bruises there.

"*Shhh.*" He rocked us gently, something that always tended to calm me down whenever I woke up from one of my nightmares.

I turned in his grip, and though it was too dark to see him, I folded in close. "I'm sorry I woke you up." The fabric against my cheek was definitely a T-shirt, his favourite piece of clothing to sleep in.

"Nothing to apologise for." His arms were still around me, his palms splayed over my back. He made me feel so calm, so good, so safe whenever we lay like this.

I hated when I woke him up with my nightmares. At the same time I was also grateful, because I didn't have to wake up on my own in a panic when the nightmares got *too* bad.

"Do you want to talk about it?"

"No." I shook my head. "It's the same. He was choking me and— well. Yeah. You know."

Damian tensed up at my words, likely because he could very well imagine it after being with me for so long. Even if he was repulsed by sex, and had never done it with anyone, it was still easy to picture.

In the beginning, before I'd properly understood

that he never wanted to have sex with anyone ever, not just me, I'd tried to push him sometimes. It never ended well. He was absolutely sure of himself, that he'd never want it, that he didn't even have a flicker of curiosity.

It had been weird to get used to the no-sex in the beginning. I'd been sexualised at a very early age—it had almost always been a part of my life. And everywhere I turned, I was bombarded with it. Everyone who was in a relationship had sex—if they didn't, something was very wrong. But we… we never had. We never would. And yet our relationship was a strong one, no matter how people kept on about how sex was an important part of an intimate relationship.

"I love you." I whispered it against his T-shirt. "I'll try not to slip up again."

"Josh." My name came out a sigh. "Don't make those kinds of promises. It only makes it worse for you when you *do* slip up."

"You think I will?"

"Yeah." Delivered in a short, clipped tone. Like he was absolutely certain of it. But I couldn't blame him. I *always* slipped up. I *always* ended up cutting myself again.

"I love you too." He pulled me in tighter. "You ready to go back to sleep? I'm knackered."

"Yeah, okay." I had no trouble with sleep. I was

half-asleep already, and with him there my night-mare faded into the background. He was safe, he was there for me, always, and he wouldn't let anything or anyone hurt me.

⁓

"I CAN'T FIND anything wrong with any of the locks." Ray brushed off his jeans as he straightened back up.

"Are you sure?" I hugged myself as I hovered near him, anxiously staring at the lock to our front door.

I'd had him check the one on the door leading outside too, but it looked all fine to him. It didn't jam or only lock halfway or anything. Neither did this one. And it was *frustrating* because I had trouble with them.

"Maybe you're not being forceful enough." He looked at me, kindly like he always did, without judgement. But then I hadn't told him exactly why I was afraid of there being something wrong with the locks.

"Maybe." But I knew they'd jammed for me earlier in the day when I'd been out to get the post. The front door, which I knew I had locked after me, hadn't been when I went back in.

Or maybe I'm just going mental.

Maybe I hadn't actually locked it. My memory wasn't the best.

"Are you all right, Josh?" Ray turned so he faced me fully, studying me.

"Yeah. Yes. Fine." But I hugged myself tighter. "I'm fine."

He gave me a small smile that clearly told me he didn't believe it for a second. "You lads are still coming for dinner tonight, yes?"

I nodded. Damian and I had said yes to that last week, when we'd also been over to theirs for dinner. I liked being there, they were such a nice family. So tight-knit. Damian was a bit of an outsider with them, but it was obvious just how much they cared about him still. And they'd welcomed me with open arms, not once questioning it.

"If there's not anything else you need, then, I have to get back to work." He studied me.

I'd rang him during his lunch break—and now here he was. Probably going over the allotted time for break, just because I'd freaked out.

"Can you check them again before you leave?" I glanced at the door. Anxiety coursed inside me. I swear someone had been watching me when I'd been outside earlier. I didn't want whoever—*I know who it is*—to be able to get in here because the locks were faulty.

He nodded, but I could tell it left him a little exasperated.

No worries, I exasperate myself. I probably worried for nothing. Everyone said he wouldn't come for me... no one seemed worried. But I *was*. And someone *had* been outside our window, someone *had* followed me, someone *was* watching me.

"Nothing wrong here." He locked and unlocked the door several times, trying it in-between. When it was locked, it stayed that day. It wouldn't open. "See?"

I nodded, not sure how I felt about it. I trudged after him out into the hall and he repeated everything with that door too. That one wouldn't budge when he locked it either.

"Maybe I forgot to lock it," I muttered, embarrassed.

"You probably did, because you see here now that once I've locked it, it can't be opened." He demonstrated again.

Humiliation seeped in. *Could I be so wrong? Could I really have forgotten to lock it?* The thing was I didn't remember. I always locked the doors after me, so it was weird I hadn't when I went out for the post.

"I'm sorry." I bowed my head.

"Don't be." He clapped my back. "It's sensible to

be afraid of this right smack in the middle of the city. There's a lot of dangerous people out there."

If only you knew.

"Don't hesitate to ring if there's anything, Josh." Now he squeezed my shoulder. "It's better to check things like this one time too many."

I managed a weak smile. "Thanks for coming."

"It's no problem." He unlocked the door and opened it. "See you at dinner later, then?"

"Yeah." As soon as the door closed behind him, I locked it. And checked three times just to make sure I really *had*. Then I hurried back into the flat and locked that door as well.

I even drew the curtains, blocking out the sun— and my view of the street. If he was out there, I didn't want to know. And I didn't want him to be able to look in on us. On me. Because I was all alone.

He's not out there. That's what Mum would say. Damian too.

But I knew better.

Or maybe I didn't.

Maybe it was my disorder. Maybe it was the borderline playing tricks on me. Maybe he had given up on me. Maybe he was out there, without plans for revenge. Maybe he was out there looking for a new kid…

Those thoughts didn't make me feel any better.

"Get up. I'm driving you to college." Andrew sat on the edge of my bed, buttoning up his shirt.

"I'll have to take a shower first." I struggled to sit up. Every single part of my body hurt.

"Hurry up, then! I don't have the whole day."

I leapt out of bed at his tone, no matter how much my body protested. I grabbed clean clothes before locking myself in the bathroom. I dropped them close to the door, turned the shower on, then stepped up to the mirror.

My razor was in the cabinet—one good thing about having my own bathroom was I didn't have to hide it. I'd turned the shower on to mask any sounds, but I still took a deep breath to try and quiet myself as I put the blade to my wrist.

Blood poured down into the sink, colouring it red. It was a calming sight. But not even this could quite make the pain of everything he'd just done to me go away. It worsened as the seconds ticked by.

I stared at myself. My eyes seemed dead, my hair was a right mess, and my skin was full of bruises from Andrew's rough treatment. *My wrists aren't enough. I need something more. More pain, more control.* Without removing my eyes from the mirror, I lifted my hand and drew a long cut down my upper arm. It didn't look like anything at first, but then the blood appeared along the line, smearing it red. Then it flowed over, trickling down my pale skin.

I watched it trickle until the first drops dripped into the sink. Then I made another one. It works. All I could feel was this pain I was causing myself, and I closed my eyes, enjoying the sting of it as I cut again and again.

"Joshua! Come on!" Andrew hammered on the door.

I jumped. "In a minute!" The razor clattered into the sink and I left it there as I dived for the shower. If I took too long, he'd punish me again, and I couldn't take it. Not today. Not tomorrow either. Not ever.

What would I have to do to see an end to this?

CHAPTER 7

"Cooper asked me out tonight."

Damian glanced at me as we walked up to the door of his uncle and aunt's house. "You should go out. Have some fun."

"You think so?" I didn't know if I was up to going out. My arm hurt, the nightmares and the memories still plagued me. I wasn't in a party-kind of mood. I wasn't even in a mood to have dinner with anyone else but Damian, but we'd already promised, so here we were.

"Yeah." He rang the bell.

"Do you want to come?" Please, say yes.

"No." He gave me an apologetic smile. I hadn't expected anything else. He didn't like to go out at all. Most I could drag him to nowadays was the pub with our mates, but definitely not out clubbing. And definitely not with Cooper. Damian wasn't much of a fan of his. Cooper was an acquired taste—one Damian had never learned to appreciate.

The door opened, revealing Claire's smiling face. "Come in! You don't have to ring the bell." She said that every time, yet Damian kept ringing it every time.

The house smelled of whatever it was she was making for dinner. Everything she made whenever we were over, was delicious. I smiled at the thought that whatever this was would as well.

Damian glanced at me, one side of his mouth twitching up a bit.

"Dinner's not quite ready. You can wait in the living room. Matilda's in there, already." She hustled into the kitchen, where I could see Ray chopping something at the counter.

Matilda was sprawled on the smaller sofa, switching through channels. She glanced up as we entered, face breaking into a smile. "Hey, you."

"Hey, Matilda." I sank down on the bigger sofa, and Damian sat down next to me, nodding in greeting to her.

The channel was on some kind of soap opera that I'd seen in my own channel-surfing , but that I didn't know anything about. Not even the name. Once she turned back to the telly, she started switching again. "There's nothing on. Evenings should be the best time for programmes, but *no*, it sucks, instead."

It didn't seem like she was talking to anyone in particular, so I refrained from answering and instead scooted a bit closer to Damian. He glanced at me, gaze searching. I tried for a smile. Keyword was *tried*, because I couldn't quite manage it. Memories and nightmares kept on repeat in my mind and my arm hurt, and I just... I just wanted to go home.

But we'd promised we'd be here for dinner, and it wasn't that often I got to meet up with Cooper—even if he now lived in London—so I *did* want to meet him, after all.

A timer rang in the kitchen, which meant that dinner would be about ready.

"I'm going to the toilet before we eat." I pushed myself up from the sofa. Damian didn't answer, just looked up at me. I managed a small smile this time before brushing past his knees.

"Would you let Matt know dinner's ready too?" Claire stuck her head out of the kitchen as I made my way past the door.

"Yeah." The toilet was on the first floor, and so was Matt's bedroom. Ray and Claire's, and Matilda's as well, for that matter. Damian had shared the basement when he lived here, along with Claire's sister, Chloe.

I headed down the hall once I'd relieved myself and washed my hands. Loud music could be heard and when I knocked on the door there was no answer. "Matt?" I tried tentatively, then raised my voice, since there was no reaction. "Matt?" Another knock. Still nothing.

Something big and ugly twisted in my stomach. If this had been me at his age, the fact I didn't answer my door was cause for worry. I'd never noticed anything about Matt, but then I hardly ever spoke to the lad.

I opened the door.

He lay flat on his bed, staring up at the ceiling. The stereo was blaring some kind of rock music that sounded vaguely familiar. What drew my eyes in the few seconds before he noticed me was his exposed wrist and the utility knife tapping lightly against it.

He sat straight upright, the knife falling to be mixed in with the sheets. The sleeve of his arm fell down to cover his skin. I wasn't sure if it hid scars or not, all I'd seen was the knife and the pale skin. At least I hadn't seen the kind of wounds and scars that I'd inflicted on myself.

His eyes were wide as he stared at me. "Josh?"

"Dinner's ready." I crossed my own arms in front

of my stomach, gripping the opposite wrists. That's where it had started for me, shallow cuts that barely bled. And it had escalated from there, too. Just look at my arms now—all skin mutilated by my own hand, by razors *I* forced down into my skin.

"I'll be right there." He looked like a deer caught in headlights. Was this how I looked when I was caught doing something I knew I shouldn't be doing?

"Matt… If you need to talk—" I was better at doing the talking than offering to be the one listening. It wasn't like I was in any sort of position to be giving advice, considering I'd just slipped up, but still… If he was doing what I was sure he was doing, then I knew exactly what it was like.

"I don't." He leaned over to turn off the stereo, which was perched on his desk, right next to the bedside table.

I'd thought so too when I was fifteen. I'd thought no one would believe me, no one would take me seriously, if I spoke up. "It helps."

Matt looked back at me, eyes hard. "I'm fine." He glanced away, then back at me again, the hardness gone. Now he was wearing a surprisingly vulnerable look. "Don't tell anyone. Please. I'm fine, it's just… I only do it sometimes. It's not deep. Please, Josh, don't tell. Not even Damian."

I didn't like it, but I nodded. I didn't want to

invade his privacy by telling someone his intimate secrets. But if he got worse... but then again, I'd never actually cut to kill—except one time—I'd cut to *live*. Because if I hadn't had my cutting, I wouldn't have survived.

Maybe it was like that for him too. Cutting seemed so bad to everyone else, but for us who did cut... it was a life-line. It kept us alive and strong and able to cope. For ten years I'd lived a nightmare—maybe even longer, but I couldn't remember so far back—and all I'd had *was* my cutting. If it hadn't been for it, I wouldn't have been alive to meet Damian.

I'd done a good job of trying to end my life five years ago, but I'd failed, and everything had turned out so much better after I'd woken up in hospital. Mum had believed me. that was all that mattered. Until I met Damian, and though he made me feel so *good*, the cutting was still a part of me. Something I still had to do from time to time to hold on to what I had.

Even after three months harm-free, I went back to it. But if I hadn't, maybe I would've done something worse. And I couldn't do that. Not to Damian, not to Mum, not to anyone.

I sunk down on the chair next to Damian, smiling faintly at him as he looked at me. Matt came shuf-

fling in after me, sleeves drawn down to his knuck-
les. I watched him without being too obvious about it
—or at least I hoped I managed not to be too obvious.

He'd always been silent and morose. He never
said much, never spoke up unless directly spoken to.
There wasn't anything different about him than usual
—except now I knew he was doing the same thing I
was still struggling with. How long had he been
cutting? Had he just started, or had it been going on
for years? *Surely not for as long as I've known him,
right?* He'd been twelve when we first met. Then
again, he could've started that young. I had. I'd been
even younger when I started.

But if it helped him, like it had me… as long as he
didn't take it too far, try to kill himself, like I had
eventually done. But then again, Matt hadn't suffered
through the hell I had. He didn't have my issues, my
diagnosis. He was a teenager—with all the normal
angst that entailed that I'd never experienced for
myself, because I'd had worse things to deal with.
Maybe it was just a phase.

He'd asked me to keep quiet, so I would. As long
as it didn't seem to go further, anyway. If he became
suicidal, then I had to tell. But for now, I'd wait and
see. It had helped me, so maybe it was helping him
too. Maybe it was what was keeping *him* alive.

CHAPTER 8

Cooper was already drunk by the time I arrived at the club. I didn't know why he'd even invited me out, because he was quite busy. Lip-locked, body-locked, whatever, with some other blond bloke.

This had been my scene once too. Years ago now, though. I hadn't been out to pull since I met Damian. The thumping music, the smoky club-scene, all the men out to pull… it wasn't my thing anymore.

I didn't miss it either. Not really.

The bar was crowded but I managed to squeeze in and order a drink. When it was put in front of me, I sipped tentatively as I glanced over at the corner Cooper was busy in. They were still lip-locked, so he had no idea I was here.

Should I go over there and interrupt? He'd asked me out, after all.

My neck prickled. I turned instantly, but I couldn't see anyone even so much as looking in my general direction. Everyone around me was busy chatting up someone else, or with more intimate things to occupy them. The bartenders were busy mixing drinks. The dance floor was packed with people rutting against each other.

But someone was watching me. I could feel it. My neck still prickled. Goose bumps ran down my spine, down my arms.

I tipped the glass to my lips, took a big swallow of it.

"Josh!" Arms wrapped around my neck. "You came!" Cooper shouted it into my ear so I'd hear him over the music.

"I said I would." I emptied the rest of my drink. The feeling of being watched was still there. It creeped me out, but that Cooper was here with me now made it a tiny bit better. "But if you're busy..." I nodded towards the blond bloke he'd been snogging, who was still in the corner of the room.

"No, that's okay." He tightened his arm around me. "Come on, I'll buy you a drink."

He did, and I drank, and the feeling of being

watched stayed with me, but the alcohol dimmed it. Eventually I forgot all about it.

Cooper might be a lot of things—untrustworthy, promiscuous, abuser of alcoholic beverages—but he always managed to get me in a good mood and to have fun.

I had no count on how many drinks I'd had. I shouldn't really have been drinking, at least not this much, but for once it felt good to let loose completely.

Bodies pressed in on all sides on the dance floor, but it didn't matter. Nothing mattered except the music and the feeling of complete abandon the alcohol had left me with.

Cooper's arms slid around my neck again, like earlier, and he leaned in to speak in my ear. "This bloke's watching us. Pretty sure he wouldn't mind a threesome right here."

I burst out laughing, because honestly… a *threesome*? With some random bloke and my *cousin*? My cousin who looked so much alike me we could've been brothers. That was probably what that bloke was thinking, too. A threesome with siblings—twins. Wasn't that a fantasy for some?

"Don't you miss it?"

"Miss what?" I hadn't been known to have threesomes, not even back at my most self-destructive.

"Sex!"

Oh. "No, not really." I thought about it, of course, but that was mostly about how it would be with Damian. But it would never happen, so it was all a fantasy. "I've had enough of that to last me a life-time." Though if Damian ever changed his mind, not that I thought he would, but *if…* I wouldn't be saying no.

Cooper shook his head. He was still leaning in close to me, arms loosely wrapped around my neck as he moved his body to the music. "I still think it's weird. Even after all these years."

"Good thing we're not all like you." I said it teas-ingly, but I did mean it. I *had* been like Cooper once upon a time, but I'd settled down. I wondered when he would settle down—if ever. I'd settled down early, before I was twenty, and he'd likely be late. If he continued like he did now he'd probably ruin his body before it even happened.

"I miss the times we went out together and pulled blokes." He smacked a kiss on my cheek. "That was good times."

It hadn't been that often, what with him living in Bristol back then. But yeah… Pulling lads hadn't ever been an issue for me back then. I hadn't even had to *try*, they'd come to me.

"I want to fuck you." The man's voice was low, intense, hoarse from all the smoke inside the club.

"As long as you've got a condom." I never had sex with anyone without protection—except Andrew, but I didn't have a say in that. But this, this was my time, my choice.

"Don't you worry, laddie, I've got everything we need." He grinned down at me. "I'm going to fuck you nice and good."

Hopefully, yes. I pushed him into the toilet stall and he reached behind me to lock the door once I was inside. His lips met mine in a hard, passionate kiss, and I returned it as I moved my hands down his body, slipping them under his shirt where they ghosted over a flat and hairy chest before going down to the hem of his trousers.

Running my hand over the front, I could feel he was already hard. I quickly, and with accustomed fingers, unzipped him.

I drew back from the kiss and wasted no time getting down on my knees. He leaned against the wall, watching me with half-lidded eyes as I pushed his trousers and pants down his thighs.

The hard length fit just right in my hand. Looking up at him, I smiled faintly, then leaned forward to get to work.

But that was years ago now. Back when I'd met Damian I'd just got through Andrew's trial, and before that hospitalisation, so I hadn't been out on the pull before I'd ended up in hospital that time. And I'd stayed in hospital for *months*.

"Hey, lads." A man sidled up to us, his muscular arms going around both our shoulders.

Cooper grinned wickedly up at him, raising an eyebrow.

It must be the bloke who'd been eying us. Or perhaps others had been too. What did I know? All I knew was I didn't like the way he leaned in, the way he grinned predatorily, the way his arm was slung so familiarly around my shoulders.

"You up for some fun?"

"Sorry, mate, we're otherwise occupied." Cooper delivered the line with utmost authority, while still maintaining that devilish grin.

"Come find me if you change your mind." The bloke winked, and it honestly looked ridiculous, but I was just relieved he'd given up so easily.

"You bet I will." Cooper turned back to face me once he danced off, rolling his eyes. "You bet I *won't*."

We headed back to the bar for more drinks. It wouldn't be long till they closed now. The few times I had been out since I met Damian, I'd never stayed until closing. That was before, when the last thing I'd wanted was to go home.

Once the bar closed, we stumbled out on the

street. Cooper didn't live all that far from us, so we headed the same way.

"Must be a change for you, going home alone for once." I buried my hands in my pocket, slouching my shoulders, as we continued along the pavement towards home.

"I don't *always* go home with someone, you know," he countered. "I am capable of spending a night in my own company. It's not as much fun, though." He grinned.

"I bet." *Or not.* I'd never had a home to bring the blokes I pulled too—we'd always had sex in clubs or pubs or in alleys, or sometimes in the home of whoever I'd been with.

"You've got someone to go home to, though. Must be nice." He sounded wistful.

I glanced over, surprised. "You thinking about settling down with someone?"

He guffawed. "Who would that be? Who'd want me, anyway?"

"Loads of people, I reckon."

He snorted in contempt.

"Oh, come on. You're great!" A bit messed up— okay, a *lot* messed up—but then who wasn't? "I found someone. If *I* can, then you definitely can." I was worse to deal with than Cooper. A sexually abused, borderline wreck. While abusing alcohol and engaging in promiscuous sex. It would be easier for him to change his ways—because I couldn't change mine. I would always be borderline. It wasn't something that would ever go away, because something was wrong in my *brain*.

"Can we talk about something else, please?" There was a whiny sound to his voice now.

I cast around for another topic, not willing to push him further. That would only lead to him turning stubborn. "Matt's cutting."

"What?"

"I saw it earlier. We went to dinner, and I think I saw cuts on his arms."

"Matt? Damian's… whatever?"

"Yeah."

"You think it's serious? Like with you?"

I chuckled, but it wasn't a happy sort of chuckle. "Not at all like me. My arms are ruined. I didn't actually see anything, just the knife he kept tapping against his wrist. But he panicked when he noticed me. So… he must be doing it."

"Teenage angst. I remember what that was like." He sighed. "Those were the days."

Hadn't his teenage days been exactly like they were now? Besides now he lived in London and not with his parents. "You're still living them, Coop. Nothing's changed, except the location."

He tilted his head from one side to the other. "Yeah, you're right."

We walked in companionable silence then, until we had to part ways.

I walked faster once I was on my own. The feeling of being watched came back, exactly like in the club, but when I cast a quick look around I couldn't see anyone. But it was dark, so… someone could be out there somewhere, without me able to see them.

I fumbled the key in the lock, but the door opened and I was quick to slip inside and shut it firmly after me. The door to the flat went easier and quicker to unlock, now I was in safety behind the locked front door.

The flat was dark and silent. I tried to be as quiet as possible as I went about drinking a glass of water, brushing my teeth, and then changing into a tee and pyjama bottoms.

Damian's breathing was deep as I lifted the duvet, but when I slid into bed next to him, he stirred. I froze, hoping I hadn't woken him up, that it was just him moving around in his sleep.

"Did you have a good time?"

No such luck. Not that I minded talking to him, of course, but I hated waking him when he was fast asleep. He needed his sleep, after all. He was the one who always had to deal with my nightmares.

"I did, yeah." I could still feel the effect of the alcohol, though the high of it had been walked off.

He rolled over to face me. One arm was slung over my chest and his cheek rested lightly against my shoulder. He was warm from sleep and I inched a bit closer, wanting to share his warmth.

Tonight's events kept rolling around in my mind, but strangely enough it wasn't the fact I'd been watched by someone that was forefront. "Hey, Damian...?"

"Hmm?"

"Do you ever think about... like, actually trying to have sex? Just to see, you know." Cooper's question of me missing it rang in my ears. I didn't exactly miss sex, what was there to miss, right? But everyone else was having it, whether they were in a relationship or not.

"We've already had this conversation," he murmured sleepily. "Several times."

"Been a while since now. Maybe you've changed your mind."

"I haven't."

Well, then. There was that issue out of the world. Was I disappointed? Relieved? Or plain old neutral? It felt like the latter. As long as I could be with him, sex didn't matter. It hadn't in the three years we'd been together, and it wouldn't start to matter now.

I settled down properly. His arm resting across my chest, and him pressed up against my side, felt so right. Even after the years we'd been together, I was still floored by the fact that I had this, that I had *him*. That he managed to live with me, that he wanted to. That I had a *relationship*, and a good one at that, after everything I'd been through.

"I'm glad you had a good time."

I tilted my head to the side so my cheek rested against the top of his. "Me too. But I feel even better being back here with you."

He chuckled, deep in his chest. "Sappy."

"What can I say, you bring it out in me." I stroked his hair lovingly.

He sighed contently. "Love you."

He was falling back asleep and I let him. My fingers still carded through his hair and I smiled to myself at the murmured words. Happiness flooded over me in such a rush I was afraid I'd drown. What we had was important, and even if other people thought it was weird, it was *ours* and it was good. Sex wasn't important. Hadn't been the last three years—and it wouldn't be.

We were important. Just the two of us.

"ood evening, Joshua."

I watched him approach with dread. I was sitting on my bed and he'd entered my bedroom, locking the door after him.

"Be a good boy tonight." He grabbed my shirt, yanking me forward so violently I would've face planted on the floor if he hadn't kept his grip on me. "Your mother's home tonight and you don't want her hearing, do you? I know I don't. So you better be quiet."

I nodded mutely.

"Not even talking to me tonight?" He pushed me back, up against the wall, and started in on my shirt. He was being unusually gentle with that. "Don't want to rip it. Wouldn't want your mother to notice anything." And there was the answer to that.

The only good thing about him coming into my room when my mother was home, was he always gentler. He wasn't violent and he didn't rip anything. It was better, of course it was, but the fact that he still came to my room... I just wished it would end.

I remained still the whole time he undressed me, standing up only so he could get my joggers and underwear off. Then I was shoved down on the bed again, face first into my pillow, and he held me down like that while he rustled with his own clothes.

I wanted to cry, to resist him, something, but I was paralysed. I couldn't do anything, my body felt like it was made of stone. Resisting never served any purpose than it hurting more, and it wasn't worth it.

Nothing was worth it. Not to go through this every single day.

Living... it simply wasn't worth it.

CHAPTER 9

*L*unch with Mum.

I needed to talk to her, to get her advice. Whatever she had to say, I needed to hear it before I rang Vincent. Maybe she knew other psychiatrists too. I wasn't quite sure if she'd got me to see Vincent because she knew about him or I'd just been lucky that very first time. I'd never asked.

I exited the lift and headed towards Mum's office. We hadn't planned lunch, but she never said no whenever I turned up. She wanted to spent as much time with me as possible, besides being at work and with her girlfriend.

Her secretary wasn't at the desk and the door to the office was half-way open, which it never was if she was in there with someone important. So I knocked and entered.

Mum stood behind her desk, her sharp gaze cutting to me as I stepped inside.

"Hey, Mum, I was—" A man had been standing with his back to me, facing Mum, but he turned now.

My stomach plummeted.

Even after three years it was impossible not to recognise him. It was impossible not to feel the terror of my childhood as I looked into that familiar face, into those cold, calculating grey eyes.

"Hello, Joshua," Andrew greeted me casually.

I stood rooted to the floor, my body frozen in shock and terror.

"Joshua." Mum came around her desk, approaching me.

That propelled me into action. I backed away, gaze flicking between them. Why was Andrew in her office? They'd been officially divorced since before the trial, so why was he *here*? Why had she let him in?

Those eyes. No remorse in them. None whatsoever.

Last time I'd seen him had been in court, when they'd read the verdict. He couldn't hurt me then, couldn't get near me, couldn't touch me. He'd been surrounded by people keeping him in place, and I had stayed as far away from him as I possibly could.

But now he was *here*, free from prison and able to go wherever he wanted. *"You are mine, Joshua. Mine and no one else's."*

I shook my head as I continued to back off. Mum came closer to me, but I flinched away from her too. "No." She'd let him in here. She'd been speaking to him. How could she do that to me?

Once I was out the door, I slammed it shut and only then did I dare turn my back. I never dared turn my back to Andrew, because he liked to attack me when I was least aware of it.

I strode back to the lift, my whole body shaking. The scars on my arms felt like they burned and I curled my hands into fists to try and restrain myself from scratching at them. Especially my left arm, which still had the sutures in.

I was an adult. I was of no interest to him anymore. I'd overcome those horrible years; I lived a happy life with the man I loved. Andrew could not do anything to ruin my life.

Except he could. The panic and the fear… it was consuming me. The memories from way back when… flooding over me.

He shouldn't be a threat anymore. He liked little boys, little boys who couldn't defend themselves. I didn't qualify anymore. He *couldn't* hurt me.

I was haunted. Haunted by the memories, they

were flashing in front of my eyes. My mind was a jumbled mess, I couldn't make sense of it. I was aware of taking the tube, of walking from the station to the flat, but my mind kept reliving my traumatic childhood, not my present.

Forgetting had never been an option. Everything he'd ever done to me— I remembered it. I didn't want to, but I did anyway. The memories pushed their way past everything that usually struggled to keep them buried far, far away. I wanted to think of my life now, with Damian... Our life together. But I couldn't muster up any kind of feeling for him because the looming nightmare of Andrew overshadowed everything else.

My fingers trembled as I made to unlock the door, and I dropped them. I stared down at them, then slowly bent to pick them up. My hands kept trembling, but this time I did manage to unlock the door.

I stumbled into the kitchen, fumbled for a glass, then turned the tap on and watched as the water sloshed down into the sink. How many times during my teenage years had I stood in the shower, letting the water pelt down on my abused skin, washing away all the blood I'd willingly drawn from my own body?

My hands were still trembling so much as I lifted the glass for a sip, that it dropped to the floor and shattered into pieces. I bent to gather the broken shards together, only to gasp in pain as the glass cut my fingers. I held my hand up so I could stare at my fingertips, where blood started to gather in small bubbles only to burst and trickle down my skin.

I could only stare at the blood. It was nothing compared to the amount of blood I used to spill. My arms could testify to that. A simple prick on the tips of my fingers was nothing compared to the countless deep scars adorning my arms. Even my scars had scars.

Letting out a shaky breath, I sat back to lean against the refrigerator. The glass was scattered around me, blood dripped from my hand. I numbly grabbed for one of the bigger pieces of broken glass, locking my hand around it. The sharp edges dug into my skin painfully and more blood trickled. It was wonderful.

When the pain had dulled, I gathered the glass I could find, scooped it up into my palms and deposited it all in the rubbish. I'd got some small cuts on my other hand as well, but it was the right one that was the issue. It was bleeding profusely.

I pushed myself up on my feet, gaze flicking nervously. I walked out of the kitchen and slipped into the bathroom. The door clicked shut behind me and I stood there, taking the space in. I slowly walked over to the sink, where I could wash all the blood off.

But emotion flooded through me again, hitting me like a tsunami crashing in on land, ruining everything in its wake. It left me staggering, arms wrapping around myself.

I needed to feel something else. I needed this to stop. More blood, more pain, anything to make it stop.

I opened the cabinet. I didn't have a razor. If I wanted to cut again, I'd have to go to the kitchen to get a knife. But the simple thought of walking anywhere, even that short a walk, left me feeling drained.

My medicine, and various over-the-counter drugs, took up half a shelf. I snagged it all, then went over to the door again, where I sank to the floor. I needed something to calm myself with. I'd taken my pills today, but I needed *more*.

I needed it all.

I took out a full tray, then slowly pressed the tablets out and onto the floor, one after another. I took a tray from the other brand too, squeezing every pill out.

I can't take it. I can't take him.

I'd done this before.

Now I was doing it again. I couldn't help myself. I

needed to stop feeling, I couldn't take being like this anymore. It was too much.

I'd stood face to face with Andrew Graham—and he hadn't been fazed at all. He'd ruined my life and he didn't *care*. I wasn't worth so much as a single piece of regret from him. If he got hold of me, he'd kill me. I'd rather do it myself. It was easier, better, without pain.

Because if he got to me, there'd be more pain than he'd ever inflicted upon me before. I knew it. I'd seen it in his eyes. The way he didn't care what he'd done —but he very much cared what *I* had done. I'd put him in prison. I'd ruined *his* life. But not half-way as much as he'd ruined mine.

I was a scarred, broken mess. It was all his fault— and he didn't care.

The two different pills had two different colours. I scooped a handful up, staring at it. A mix of pink and white. A mix I took every day. Just not this many.

They called to me though, like this was meant to happen. Like it wasn't an act of impulse. I was acting on impulse, I knew it… but I couldn't stop it. I kept seeing his eyes, those cold, grey eyes— no remorse, no nothing. He was a cold-hearted psychopath. He had ruined my life, he had ruined *me*.

He finally succeeded in what he'd always tried to do; break me. I was shattered, as shattered as that glass I'd dropped. That was me. Thrown in the rubbish. Replaceable. A shattered glass couldn't be put together, just like I couldn't be put together again. Broken beyond repair.

I was tired of fighting. Done with it. I couldn't do it anymore. I was absolutely, truly *done*.

After years and years on medicine, I had no trouble swallowing pills dry. So that's what I did.

FIVE YEARS AGO

The bathroom door was securely locked. My razor was on the sink and I searched through the cabinets in a frenzy, grabbing all the pills I could find. Anything would do, as long as it worked. It had to work.

I collapsed on the floor in a fit of sobs, but managed to crawl up into a sitting position. I started opening the pill-cases, popping the pills so they spilled into a pile in front of me.

I reached out for the bottle I'd brought with me. Vodka. Nice, strong alcoholic beverage that would make this so much easier. I took a sip, preparing myself, and it burned down my throat. Next I popped pills into my mouth, took another sip to wash them down with.

When all the pills were gone, I started to feel it. Dizzy, like the world couldn't stand still anymore. I fumbled up on the sink for my razor, yanked my sleeves up, and put the blade to skin. I pressed it down deep and dragged it backwards, up towards my elbow.

This was the way, to cut vertical, along the main artery. This was the way to truly bleed.

When the right hand was bleeding profusely, I did the same on the left, only slower this time as my already hurt hand protested the movement.

My strength was leaving me, from the tablets, from the blood, and I couldn't keep my hand up anymore. It fell limp to my side, the razor cluttering against the tiles. I tipped forward, forehead pressed against the fluffy rug.

I gasped in a breath as darkness came lurking.

The last thing I thought was, *please let me die*.

PART II
STALKER

Noun.
a person who pursues game, prey, or a person
stealthily.

CHAPTER 10

Loud voices, blinking lights, something moving—
Blackness, more light, more high voices. Darkness
again, but something was still moving. Someone
yelled. Shook me. And then… nothing at all.

I woke up slowly. The light hurt my eyes as I tried
to blink them open, so I quickly closed them again.
My whole body felt heavy, like it was weighted down
by something heavy.

A *beeping* sound penetrated my groggy brain. Was
that our alarm? No. That one was louder, shriller.
Besides, Damian never let it ring long enough to
wake me up. Not when he had school. Because he
had, right?

My mouth was dry, sore. The *beeping* continued.
My body didn't cooperate. I inched my eyelids open,

taking in the pale room. I turned my head a bit on the pillow and found Damian slumped in a chair.

His eyes were closed, his arm perched on the arm of the chair and hand cupping his cheek. He looked drawn, exhausted.

"D-Damian?" My voice was hoarse and sore too. It hurt to speak. It rasped. *What happened? Why am I in hospital?*

He jerked, eyes flying open. He was out of the chair and at my side in a second. "Josh?"

"W-what h-happened?" It *really* hurt to speak.

"You don't remember?" His gaze turned sharp, narrowing.

Remember? What was I supposed to remember? I couldn't think. My brain was mush.

"Josh. You did this. You overdosed."

Oh. Right. Why? Because of Andrew. His face flashed in my mind, the cold eyes who didn't hold a hint of remorse. "No. No." I didn't want to see him, to remember him. I wanted to forget, to escape—

"What? Josh?" Damian's hand clamped down on my shoulder.

"A-Andrew." It hurt just as much to swallow as to speak.

Damian's expression turned tense. "Angie said you met. In her office."

I nodded, my throat hurting too much to speak. I

lifted my hand, the one not with an IV attached to it, to touch my neck. Damian's gaze followed my movement.

"They had to pump your stomach. Don't you remember the last couple of days?"

"S-should I?" I'd been out for a couple of *days*?

"You've been awake, Josh." He took a deep breath, straightened up, like he was worried about what he was gong to say next. "You've been halluci- nating. You haven't been able to move your feet. You've been out of it—but you've been awake, too. God." He dragged his hand over his face, eyes moist. "I've been so worried. They didn't know if you'd ever get back to yourself again."

I swear I stopped breathing for a second there. "What'd you mean… like brain damage?"

His eyes were haunted now as he gazed down at me. "Yeah. That was a distinct possibility. Do you know how lucky you are?"

I didn't feel lucky. I didn't feel anything but the pain and the heaviness. Everything *hurt*. "He s-stood there. Facing me. And there was nothing… not a twinge of regret. He doesn't think he's done anything wrong." He ruined my life, and yet he stood there, looking at me like we were old acquaintances. Like the simple sight of him didn't drag me back into the nightmare I'd been in for all my life.

"Of course he doesn't. Else he wouldn't have done what he did for ten years." Damian leaned down, hand still clamped tight on my shoulder as his cheek brushed mine. "You shouldn't be thinking about him. Yes, he's out, but he's on licence. He's not going to come near you. Meeting him in your mum's office… that was just a coincidence. If she'd known you were coming, she never would've asked him to meet her there."

Mum asked him to meet her. "Why? Why did she want to meet with him?"

"She wanted to make sure he knew that you were off limits. That he wasn't to get anywhere close to you again." Damian's arms slid around me—or my neck, as I was still lying flat on the bed. "God, Josh. I've been so worried. Why didn't you come to me instead of doing what you did?"

I honestly didn't know why I'd done it. I'd wanted to get away, from him, from my emotions. And the tablets had been a way of achieving that. I hadn't even stopped to think what it would do to him. *Oh god.* "D-did you f-find me?" I hadn't done that to him, had I? Let him find me lifeless on the bathroom floor?

He shook his head, his stubbled cheek rasping against my own stubble. "Your mum chased after you. She found you, likely right after you'd lost consciousness. If you'd been lying there longer, then the prognosis would've been even more dire than it was to begin with."

I lifted my hands, clutching at his shirt, bunching the material in my fists. "I'm so sorry." I had wanted to die, but I didn't actually *want* to die. Not really. I wanted to be with him. We had a good life.

He didn't say anything, just clutched me in return.

I didn't know how long we stayed like that. It could've been minutes, or hours. The feel and smell of him was all that mattered to me. I heard the click of heels, but didn't register it before I heard the rustle of clothes nearby.

My eyes inched open and I saw Mum standing in the doorway, face set in a grim expression as she gazed at me and Damian. "M-Mum."

Damian startled and lifted back up, but his hand stayed on my shoulder even as he turned to face her. I was grateful. It gave me comfort, it felt safe.

"Joshua?" She took a couple steps closer to the bed. "How are you?"

I wanted to tell her I was fine, because she looked so drawn and worried, but I *wasn't*. I couldn't lie. "I don't know."

A sound left her, it sounded close to a sob, and then she was the one hugging me tight. "I'm so sorry,

Joshua. I never should've had him meet me in the office. I never should've met with him at all. I just wanted to—" Her voice broke, and that startled me more than anything. I'd seen Mum cry before, when she told me about her own abuse at the hand of her own father, but never seen or heard her lose control of her emotions like this. "I wanted to make sure he'd leave you alone. I can't stand the thought of him getting to you again. If he does, he'll have to serve out the rest of his prison sentence. He doesn't want that."

The dark shadow outside our living room window flashed in my mind. She didn't know Andrew—not like I did. And Andrew would want revenge. I knew it. But I didn't say it. They, or Mum anyway, seemed set on the fact he wouldn't risk going back to prison.

"What happens now?" I wanted to go home with Damian, but I knew that wouldn't be on the cards anytime soon. Not after something that so very clearly was a suicide attempt. And if I'd been so out of it for the past couple of days I couldn't remember it… well.

"They're keeping you here for observation," Damian said. "As for after that…" He trailed off. He didn't have to continue. Another hospitalisation, that's what would happen. They couldn't force me, not really, but I'd go along with it. Hospitalisations had helped in the past. It'd been months since the last one—and now I was back to being a wreck again.

But hospitalisation was good for helping with that. It always had before. But Andrew hadn't been out on the streets watching me before either. I knew he was. He had to be. Who else would be watching me, right?

Mum let go of me almost hesitantly and straightened up. She smoothed her shirt down, schooling her face back into the neutral expression it normally wore.

I looked up at Damian. He was gazing down at me.

Please don't leave me. The words popped into my mind. Needy... I knew. I also knew he wouldn't leave. After all these years, after dealing with me for so long... he wouldn't. And if I ever thought he would, it was because of my disorder. I didn't have count on how many times he'd told me that.

"You should go home." He looked exhausted. "Get some sleep. A shower. Rest." I wanted him to stay with me, of course I did, but he needed sleep and rest. I didn't want him exhausted just so he could sit and hold my hand. I could manage on my own. I was in a hospital, it wasn't like I could do anything stupid again, not here.

Damian didn't like that idea.

"I can stay." Mum glanced between us. "He's right, Damian. You do need sleep. In your own bed. You've been here since Joshua was admitted."

A couple of days. Jesus. I squeezed my eyes shut. My body still felt all heavy, my throat still hurt. No wonder if they'd had to pump my stomach. What had Damian said? I hadn't been able to feel my legs… I tried wriggling them and they moved, so I felt them fine now.

Damian relented. I could tell from the way his shoulders fell a tiny fraction. He leaned down, kissed my forehead. "You sure?"

"Yeah." Absolutely sure. "Go home."

"Do you need me to bring anything for when I come back?" He ran his hand through my tangled hair. It probably looked horrible. Tangled and unwashed for so long.

"My journal? And iPad? With the keyboard." I'd like my laptop, but the iPad was easier to handle. I could do what I needed on it, anyway.

He kissed my cheek now, lingering before straightening up. "If you want me to come back, just ring, okay?"

I nodded, though I knew I wouldn't. I knew I was selfish sometimes, like when I'd woken him up after learning that Andrew was out of prison, just so he could comfort me. But he needed his sleep and I was going to let him have it. Now, at least. This time.

He seemed torn, then bent down for another hug. "I love you," he whispered into my ear.

"I love you too." More than I could ever articulate or explain or show. I could only say it and hug him tight and hope he understood just how deep that feeling went.

I woke up to bright lights. To beeping. To a sore throat and to pain in my arms. On my arms. Whatever. I woke up to a whispered conversation going on at my bedside.

Glancing over, I saw Mum and Grandma standing close. What was Grandma doing here? I didn't remember anything about neither her nor Mum mentioning she was coming down to visit.

Even my eyes hurt, but I forced my gaze away from them to look down on myself. Something was taped to my hand. No, a syringe or whatever it was called was piercing my skin and taped to it.

And then... bandages. Covering my entire forearms.

Oh god. "No. No."

I wasn't aware I'd spoken until they'd both turned towards me, saying my name in unison.

Tears rose and leaked over. "No." Why? "Why didn't it work?" Why was I still here? "Why am I still alive?"

"Joshua!" Grandma sounded scandalised. "Don't say something like that!"

I closed my eyes. I didn't want to see them or the hospital room or the bandages that showed how clearly I'd failed to do the one thing I'd absolutely wanted to do.

A sob left me, and once it had been set in motion, I couldn't stop. My chest hurt from it, yet I couldn't stop.

"I'll go get the doctor." That was Mum, speaking for the first time.

I wanted to rip out the needle in the back of my hand. I wanted to rip open the bandages and tear out the stitches that must be holding my skin together. I wanted to bleed out, I wanted to die!

Why couldn't they understand? Why'd they take me here? Why'd they let them save me? "I d-didn't want to b-be s-s-saved!" Everything hurt, not just my body, but inside too. The inside hurt so much, so much more than anything on the outside could ever hurt me, and I wanted it to stop. I needed it to stop!

"I don't want to be alive!" I reached over with my

free hand and ripped the needle out. It hurt, but if there was anything I was used to, it was pain. Physical pain was nothing. Nothing at all. "I don't want to live!"

"Joshua!"

"No!" Blood trickled from where I'd ripped the needle out. It was stark red against my pale skin. Fascinating. Addicting. It was how I was supposed to die. Bleeding out. I had planned it, I had done it, and I'd failed at it.

Hands touched me and I jerked away from them. I didn't know if they were Grandma's or if Mum had come back with the doctors. All I knew was I hadn't managed to finish what I'd started, and that I did want to finish it.

I couldn't stay alive. Couldn't. I couldn't go back. Go back there, to him. I just couldn't. Dying was the better option, the only option, the one I preferred. I didn't have anything or anyone to live for. I wanted only death.

And then all went dark.

CHAPTER 11

*E*mptiness. Anxiety. A need to *feel*. To press a blade into my skin, to split it apart and watch the blood trickle. To feel the *pain*. Fear. All-consuming fear. But how I could feel pain and emptiness at the same time was beyond me.

"Hi, Josh."

I pushed up on my elbows at the familiar voice. "Silver?" He strode into the room with confidence, wearing loose-fitting jeans and a vest. His arms were completely on display, with the fit biceps and the tattoos.

"How are you feeling?" He sat down on the chair next to my bed, eyes studying me.

Like with Mum and Damian, Silver was someone else I couldn't lie to. He'd been there from the beginning. Damian's flatmate and best friend. He'd been there through everything Damian had been there through, and he was supportive. He'd never warned Damian off me, not that I knew, anyway. "Not all that good."

His gaze didn't leave my face. "What happened?"

"Didn't Damian tell you?" We *lived* together, sure Damian must've shared what had happened with him. He and Silver were best mates, they knew each other and they shared things with each other.

"I want to hear it from you."

Oh. Okay. That was fair. "I saw him. Met him. Looked right into his eyes."

Silver didn't need me to explain who *he* was. *He* was someone who was well-known in my circle of friends. And Damian had already told him.

"I can't even imagine how that must've been for you."

No, he couldn't. I stared down at my hands. I was in a tee, not that stupid hospital gown, so my mutilated skin was on full display. Only thing wrapped up was my right hand.

"Where's Kian?"

"Shift at work. He says hi."

I nodded. Work was a perfectly good excuse to not come to visit. Damian only had school. This was his day of quitting early, so he should've been here already. But he wasn't.

"What's wrong?" Silver raised his eyebrows in question.

"Damian hasn't been here today. He was supposed to come after school, but it's hours since it finished, and I haven't heard anything." My hands clenched into fists. "Maybe he's done with me. Maybe he's tired of all this."

"You honestly think that?"

"Yeah. No. Yes." He always kept his promises. But not today. And I was empty and anxiety-ridden and scared. Scared that this was the last straw, that he'd had enough.

"Josh. You know that's bullocks. That's you being insecure. Afraid of abandonment. But you know better than to listen to those feelings."

Silver was quoting Vincent's words. I didn't have count on how many times Vincent had said that to me. Likely hundreds of times in the five years he'd been my psychologist.

"I hope he'll be here soon."

"He will be." Silver abandoned the chair to sit on the edge of my bed.

I leaned forward to rest my head on his shoulder. My hospitalisations were either because I was depressed and suicidal or because I just needed the break, because my feelings were so difficult to deal with. This was only the second time I'd been sectioned after a suicide attempt though. It'd been six years since the first time I'd attempted one.

"What happened to your hand?" He touched the bandage gingerly.

"Broken glass." None of the cuts had been so deep I'd needed sutures, which I suppose was a good thing. But if I could've chosen between cutting so deep I'd need sutures or swallowing pills, I knew which one I'd choose now. Too bad I wasn't able to think clearly when my feelings overwhelmed me, which they constantly did. Medicine did help, but not always.

"I never should've swallowed all my pills," I muttered, guilt washing over me. "Meeting him... I got completely out of control. It was the only option. I couldn't— couldn't stop it. I didn't want to. I wanted to die so I didn't have to see those eyes, see how he felt *nothing*. No regret, no guilt, no shame. He ruined me. And he doesn't *care*."

"Psychopaths don't." He patted my head. "You should just say *fuck you* and live your life. Because no matter what he did, it didn't stop you from actually having a life now. Having a boyfriend who loves you. But I know it's easy to say it and not so easy to do it."

It wasn't easy at all.

There was a knock on the door, at the same time as a familiar voice said, "Am I interrupting?"

"Damian!" I looked up, a wide smile spreading along with the utter relief that started in my stomach and spread out.

"I'll be taking my leave then." Silver stood up, brushing down his jeans before grinning at me.

"You'll come back to see me, right?" We lived together, but I didn't know how long I'd have to stay in the hospital.

"Of course I will. Kian will join me next time, too." He patted Damian's shoulder, muttered something, then waved to me as he exited my room.

"I didn't know he was coming to visit." Damian came over to me.

"Me neither. He just showed up earlier. Nice surprise." I smiled tentatively up at him, nervousness ratcheting up again. He looked tired. But tired of what? Me? My situation? "Are you all right?"

"Yeah. Just got held back at school." He finally leaned down to kiss me and the nervousness evaporated. He wouldn't kiss me if he was done with me, would he? But he wasn't. Silver had been right—he'd been caught up with something at school.

"I'm sorry."

He eyed me curiously. "For what?"

"I didn't think you'd show up." I pressed my lips together and stared down at my hands. I wasn't good at lying, and besides, ever since I started therapy, honesty was recommended. "That you wouldn't come back."

"Josh." He sunk into the chair with a sigh. "I was held up. If I could've left when class was over, I would've. There's nothing I want more than to come here and be with you. You know that."

"Yeah." I nodded, ashamed. Of course I knew that. *Now.* When he was with me. It was when he wasn't, when I was in bed all alone in a hospital that the doubts came creeping in. They never did when I was at home, but here... here everything was different. I did like being here, to get better, but I didn't like the feelings that overcame me *all the time.* "I hate being like this." Borderline... If only I hadn't been I would've had a normal range of emotions, not the intense, all-consuming ones I was living with now.

No one else ever reacted quite to the extent to things the way I did. I noticed it, how different I was. Especially from Damian, who was always so calm. And I was never calm, I was always tied up in some intense feeling. Or the emptiness. Though I didn't feel that often when he was around. He never made me feel empty. He always made me feel loved and appreciated and like I mattered.

"It's who you are." He stood from the chair again and came over to wrap his arms around me, pulling me in against him. I rubbed my nose against his neck, settling in comfortably. He smelled of his usual cologne. I loved that smell, it was so familiar. It was *him*.

"I'm so lucky to have you." Someone more impatient wouldn't have bothered with me, not in the long run. But he was cool, aloof, centred. Sure of what he wanted. We were so very different—and the cliché was right, because for us, opposites really did attract.

"You know I'll come by every day you're in here. I always do. It's not a chore for me. I want to keep you company." His hands stroked my back in soothing circles. "I'll always be here, even if I have to miss school. You're more important."

It was sweet of him. But school was also important. I supported him in his choice, I really did. He wanted to be a surgeon and he was working on achieving that dream.

"I'm so proud of you." It came out muffled, as my face was buried in his neck.

"And I am of you."

Now that I didn't believe. "You can't be. Not *now*."

"I am, Josh. No matter what, I am proud of you,

because you're still here, you're still fighting, you're still living. You want to live."

Yeah, because I wanted to be with him. I couldn't die—not while he was around. He was everything to me.

"And you're everything to me."

Oops. I hadn't realised I'd muttered that one aloud. But what did it matter? Those were the words I wanted to hear.

I smiled and scooted in closer. His arms tightened around me. All bad feelings were forgotten. All was wonderful.

FIVE YEARS AGO

I was awake and calm. Instead of fighting it once I woke up again, I'd decided to just lay there, completely still and silent. Once they left me alone, or once they discharged me, I'd do another try. This time I would succeed.

Mum was sitting in the chair at the side of my bed, after having relieved Grandma so she could go home and sleep. Mum was reading some case-file. I supposed she was busy at work. She always was.

If I died... then she'd be alone. Alone with Andrew. And I *was* going to die. But she should know what kind of monster she lived with, that she was married to.

"He's a sick, perverted, paedophile."

"What?" She was distracted, like she didn't even

137

properly listen to my words. That was nothing new, it was normality. Mum was always busy. Andrew had "sacrificed" his own career, staying in the same boring job for all these years with no ambition. Because of her. Yeah, right. Because if she was busy, he could get busy with me.

"Andrew is."

"Why do you say that?" Still distracted, like my words weren't worth her full attention. Well, they would now.

"He rapes me. He's been raping me for as long as I can remember."

She'd been rustling papers, but now it stopped.

"When I was younger, I used to be terrified of nights. Because that was when he came into my room and into my bed. As I got older, it didn't happen just at night. Now it happens everywhere. My room, living room, bathroom, your room. Wherever he wants. He does whatever he wants. Has his way with me, hits me, beats me, whips me. Forces me to go down on him when fucking me isn't enough for him."

She drew in a sharp breath. "Joshua—"

"You were always so busy. There were so many times I tried to tell you, but you were busy. You didn't have the time. Work always came first. And he, the kind, dedicated husband, gave you the chance to further your career while he stayed at home to watch over your kid." A bitter laugh escaped me. "Yeah, right. It was exactly what he wanted. To have me all to himself." I bit my bottom lip, thinking back. "So that's who you're married to. That's who you'll be left with when I die."

"You're not going to die."

"I am. I might've survived this time, but I'll keep trying. I can't be watched all the time. I'll manage it. Some way or another, even if I have to jump in front of a car or off a bridge. Or from my bedroom window. I'll manage it. I'll die. And you'll be left with your sick, sadistic, paedophile of a husband. Good luck pleasing him."

Done. I had nothing more to say. Now she knew.

Silence was all that met me too. I was silent, she was silent. We were both sitting there in silence. Well, technically, I was lying down. In silence.

Then Mum gathered her papers together and stood. Her heels clacked against the floor as she left the room, not having spoken another word to me.

Well, that was that. She didn't believe me.

I'd thought… well, no, not really. Hoped maybe. I'd hoped that maybe she did care about me, deep down, even if she'd never had much to do with me all my life. But no… she didn't.

Now I definitely had no reason to live. She didn't

believe me, Andrew would never admit to what he'd been doing to me... and I couldn't go back to it. Dying, it was so final. Nothing could hurt me then. I'd know nothing. I would be at peace.

I just wanted to be at peace. Why was everyone stopping me from getting some peace, after not having had it for my entire life?

CHAPTER 12

*R*ay and Claire's hallway was usually so bright and welcoming whenever we were over. It didn't seem that way now. It hadn't changed or anything, but it was me. Everything seemed so *dark*.

Damian led me down to what had been his bedroom when he'd still lived at home with them. It was still his bedroom, because it wasn't like they'd done anything to it.

I deposited my bag on the bed and turned to him. He was studying me.

"You sure you're okay staying here?"

I nodded jerkily. "I am." It was either here or go down to Bristol to stay with Grandma. I loved her, but I'd rather stay close to Damian and Mum and everyone else I knew.

He came over, hands clamping down on my shoulder. "I don't want to get rid of you, you know that, right?"

We'd already had this conversation when he'd aired the idea of me staying here as an alternative to Mum making me go to Bristol. But I couldn't blame him for saying so again—my constant neediness and fear of abandonment made me do stupid things. Like the thing I'd now finally been released for doing, after weeks in hospital.

"I know." I did. I did know that. Of course I did.

He kissed my forehead, hands moving up to stroke my cheeks. "Unpack your stuff. Rest up. They'll leave you alone as long as you're down here. Claire'll let you know when there's dinner."

Another jerky nod.

"I'll be back tonight." He had to go back to school. There was something he couldn't miss. A test or something.

"Yeah."

"I love you." He kissed my cheek this time, arms going around me in a hug.

"You too."

"Bye."

The word stuck in my throat. He smiled. I tried,

but didn't manage it. He left. I stood there rooted to the floor.

My bag was still on the bed. I stared at it, then walked over and zipped it open. Clothes, socks, underwear. My electronic devices. All I'd need to stay with Ray and Claire. In Damian's old room. *Old.* Me here, alone, without him. Because he had school and he had the flat, and I was relocated here because no one trusted me.

"It would be best for you, Joshua. At least for a little while."

They didn't trust me on my own. The thought saddened, then angered me. It rose up like a tsunami and crashed against land, wrecking everything it came over.

The bag skidded off the bed, landing heavily on the floor next to it. I stared down at it, breathing heavily. The fight had already gone out of me, leaving me feeling hopeless. I sank onto the bed, fell onto my side, and curled up.

Tears leaked, and I wasn't able to stop them. Why would I? Everything really was *hopeless*. I was alive, I was alone, I was a failure, Andrew was out to get me—and there was nothing I could do about any of it.

That was the reason I agreed to stay here, because Andrew was out there. He knew where I lived, but surely he couldn't know where Damian's uncle and aunt lived, right? Or did he?

My chest tightened to the point it hurt. What if he did know? What if he kept following me around?

Terror. That's what it was. I was terrified. Always had been. Always would be.

How could he be out! They should throw him back in prison again. That's where he belonged. He didn't belong out here.

Maybe I didn't either. My fingers itched to scratch at my arm, to hold a razor, to press it down. But I didn't have any with me and I doubted there'd be one in the bathroom here in the basement. It was only in use whenever Damian or Chloe stayed over, and that didn't happen often.

I jumped approximately three feet in the air when something jumped half on the bed, half on me. Sitting up right, terrified, I got a pink tongue in my face and small paws scratched against my chest.

"What the—" I grabbed the little fur-ball around its waist and held it out, staring at it.

It was a *dog*. And it seemed to be smiling at me, tongue hanging out, as it squirmed in my grasp. It was a funny looking dog. Its eyes were two different colours, one blue and the other brown. Its nose was two different colours too, pink and black. And the fur... there was a lot of white, but also mottled patches of black and grey and even some brown. Or was it called red when it came to a dog's fur colour? I had no experience with dogs whatsoever.

I let it go and it came scratching back, tongue licking over my neck and jaw, wherever he could reach.

"Friendly fella, aren't you?" I petted him. Or her.

The puppy wore a collar around its neck, almost hidden by the fluffy fur. There was one of those tags shaped as bones with a name on it. *Storm*. That was usually a boy's name, wasn't it? So the dog was a male.

I scratched his neck, behind his ear. He leaned into it, eyes closing, tongue still lolling out.

A smile spread on my lips. "You're sweet." Funny-looking, cuddly, sweet.

The despair of moments ago were gone, replaced by immediate affection for this little fur-ball that seemed to like me in return.

I lay back down again, but didn't curl up this time. Instead I lay on my back, with the little puppy laying over my stomach and chest, eyes still closed in enjoyment as I petted him.

It was relaxing to have him there, to feel the soft fur against the palm of my hand.

We both fell asleep like that, because the next thing I knew there was a soft knock on the door. It wasn't closed completely, there was a small opening where the puppy had managed to sneak in earlier.

"Yeah?" I sat up, crossed my legs, and rubbed my eyes. The puppy blinked his eyes where he lay on his side, then he stood and shook himself.

The door pushed open and Claire stepped over the threshold. Her eyes immediately fell on the puppy. "So this is where she ran off to." She smiled at me. "Dinner's ready, if you're up for it."

The dinner information registered at the back of my consciousness somewhere, because the pronoun she used to the puppy took all my attention. "She?"

"Yeah."

"I thought— the name Storm. I thought it was a he."

"Matt named her." Claire came closer and leaned down to scratch Storm behind her ear.

"I didn't know you were getting a dog."

"It's Matt's really, he's the one who wanted one." Her smile turned a bit tighter now.

I wondered if she knew about Matt's cutting. Was that why he'd got a dog? Had he promised to stop if he did? Or did they hope he would? But he'd been so adamant about me not telling anyone... I didn't think he would come clean on his own. Maybe they'd caught him.

A month long stay in hospital was not good for

keeping up to date with everyone. Damian wasn't someone who gossiped either—though this would be information, not gossip. Maybe he didn't know either. He wasn't exactly an open person and he didn't see his uncle and aunt *that* often. Mostly only for the times we came to dinner and the odd weekend.

"Anyway." She straightened. "There's dinner. Are you up for it?"

I wasn't. Not before the fur-ball. Or before our nap. "Yeah."

Dinner with Damian's family, also part of mine now since we were together, did sound nice.

While I followed Claire upstairs, Storm followed in my heels. Ray and Matilda were already sitting at the table, laughing at something one of them had said. Matt came shuffling in, looking worse for wear than I did at the moment. Then again, I'd been in the hospital recuperating for a month, so I wasn't doing so bad compared to when I tried to kill myself.

I hoped Matt wouldn't get to that. To the suicide attempt. Or worse, succeed at it.

But then Matt saw Storm, and he finally smiled as he bent down to pet her.

So maybe he'd be okay after all. He seemed generally happy with Storm—it was everything else that seemed to make him miserable.

Maybe a dog was a good idea. He had someone to depend on, someone besides his family. I had Damian, though again… that wouldn't stop me if I fell down that black hole again and all that could stop the pain and the misery was a knife or pills. Not even a dog could stop me if it happened. The impulsiveness… it was never a good quality, especially not when I was so far down.

I was still alive, though. And that was a good thing.

CHAPTER 13

*R*ay and Claire's living room had big windows as well as a glass door leading out to the garden. They had a big garden, lots of lawn and a couple trees at the edge. Claire had flowerbeds out there too, in full bloom. All kinds of colours. It was beautiful.

Storm ran around the grass, jumping, rolling, and all around enjoying herself. I sat on the veranda stairs, watching her. She was so young, so full of life, so full of *enjoyment*. I'd never been like that. Maybe when I was a toddler, in kindergarten, before I learned how shit the world and people could be.

How nice wouldn't it be to be a dog? No worries. Always happy to see their owner. To be so loved and cuddled and cared for. *No worries...* That would be nice. To live in the here and now, too. Wasn't that what dogs did? They didn't dwell on the past. To them, it was the here and now that mattered.

I wish I could live in the here and now, to put my past behind me. Wouldn't that be nice? To stop dwelling on all that happened, to stop having it destroy me and ruin my life.

Storm stopped suddenly, head turned toward the trees at the furthest side of the garden, ears standing up. I followed her focus, squinting. It was already twilight and in the shadow of the trees… I couldn't see anything, but Storm could see or hear something, and I felt cold all over.

I scrambled back up the stairs. "Storm, come here." Her head turned slightly, but then it turned back, ears still standing up.

My shoes slid on the wood, and I turned and stumbled back inside. Matt was there, staring at me as I struggled to stay on my feet.

"You have to call her in. She can't stay out there."

"Why not?"

"He's out there!" I scooted sideways, hiding in front of the curtains so he couldn't look in the big windows and see me.

"Who's out there?" Matt eyed me.

"Get her inside!" Storm couldn't stay out there! Not when he was there. And he was, I knew he was.

She'd sensed him or heard him or smelled him or *something*. He was here, watching me.

Matt continued to eye me for another couple seconds, then he stepped out to call Storm inside. She came when it was him calling, shooting inside like a rocket, and ending up sliding on the floor, almost losing her footing. Kinda like me, moments before.

"I don't see anyone out there, Josh." Matt came in, closing the door behind him.

"He is. He's there. Hiding and watching. I know he is." I always knew when he was close. And he bloody well *was*. If I wasn't even safe her, in a house with a big garden, outside of London, then where was I safe? *Maybe I should've gone down to Bristol after all*. Surely he wouldn't be desperate enough to follow me there. *Oh yes, he would*. "You have to lock the door." I didn't move, just stared from the door to Matt.

Matt stared back, blinking, lips slightly parted.

"Lock the door!" Open doors were so easier to get through than locked ones. Though a locked door wouldn't stop him if he did want to come in. Especially not when it was all glass. "Lock it!"

"Okay, okay." Matt held his arms up, palms out, then did as I demanded. "There. It's done. But I still don't see anyone out there."

"He's good at hiding." I dared to lean over and

look out. Didn't see anything. Straightened back up in front of the curtains. There was a window on the other side of me, also a lot of glass he could look in through.

"Josh?"

I couldn't stay here. Trapped in between a window and a door. And he out there, watching.

"Josh?"

There was a straight route to the hallway and then down to the basement. He'd see me through the bloody windows, but it would only take me a few moments to reach the basement and then he couldn't see me anymore.

"Josh?"

I ran for it. The stairs seemed to shake beneath my frenzied need to get downstairs. Damian's room was a safe haven, it was in the basement, no wind—

No! There were two windows. Not as big as the living room, but enough to get out of if there should be a fire or some other need to climb out. They faced the other side of the house, not where I knew Andrew had been.

I jerked the curtains closed on both windows. Then snuck my hand in-between them to check that they really were locked. If I could get out through those windows, he could get in.

Once I was sure no one could see in, I sat down

on the bed. My hands rested in my lap, twisting anxiously together. I was wound tight, unable to relax. Panicking. Terrified.

Someone descended the stairs. I could hear the steps creak under the person's weight. It definitely wasn't the puppy: either I wouldn't hear it or I would hear the clacking of claws.

"Josh?"

The voice washed over me, calming the worst of the anxiety.

Damian entered the room, rucksack slung over one shoulder before he deposited it on the floor next to the door. He only had eyes for me, discarding the rucksack without a single glance. He came to crouch in front of me, enveloping my trembling hands in his.

"Matt said you were freaking out."

It was time to tell. Time to tell him I was being stalked. "He's out there, Damian. He's following me. Watching, biding his time."

Damian sighed, glanced down, then met my gaze again. "He's not. Josh… He's not."

"Yes, he is." I knew with certainty. I knew Andrew, better than anyone. He *was* out there. He *was* coming for me.

Damian shook his head. "Why would he risk it?"

"Revenge."

"Josh." My name came out on another sigh. "Don't you think you're being a little paranoid?"

I drew in a sharp breath. "Don't you think you're being a bit too relaxed?" I snapped, then instantly regretted it. "I'm sorry." I couldn't snap at the person who dealt with me on a daily basis. He'd stayed with me three years—I wanted it to be three more. A lot longer than that, too. If he left me… then what did I have?

He released my hands and instead cupped his over my cheeks. "There wasn't anyone outside."

"There *was*. I know there was. Storm knew someone was there too. Someone drew her attention."

"That could've been anything. Dogs have better hearing than us. It could've been a bird or rustling of leaves. It's windy outside."

"Why won't anyone believe me? I know he was there! He's been stalking me." I stared at him, willing me to understand. "Someone was standing outside or flat looking in one night. Two times I've been followed when I was out. I didn't see anyone then either, but I *know*— I *know* he was there. Damian…"

Why couldn't he understand?

"Just because he's out of prison, he's not out to get you." His thumbs stroked my cheeks. "I think we should take a nap. Perhaps you'll feel calmer and more rational once you've had some sleep."

He didn't understand. He *wouldn't* understand.

"Okay. Yeah." At least he was here. I wasn't alone. That was something, at least.

FIVE YEARS AGO

Only a few minutes after Mum had left, there he was. Standing in the doorway, hard eyes focused on me.

My breath stuttered, stopped. My chest, my stomach, my arms hurt just from looking at him.

"Joshua."

I couldn't speak. All I could do was stare at him, at how he slowly pushed off the doorway and stepped into the room. He turned—I hoped maybe he'd leave—but he only closed the door.

No, no, no. He couldn't do anything here! I was in a hospital. There were people here, doctors and nurses, and Mum must still be somewhere— maybe she'd known. Maybe she'd left the room so he could get some time with me.

Had she known all this time, through all these years?

"What've you done?" He came up to the bed, hands running over the back of it, slipping down to the duvet, close to my foot.

I jerked my foot away.

Why was he here? How dared he come after me in a hospital?

What if no one came to look in on me? Grandma had gone home to sleep. She wouldn't be back for hours. Mum... she'd walked out. She hadn't said a word. She might not have known, but there was also the possibility that she did know. *What if she does? What am I going to do then?*

Die... that was all I wanted to do. But I wanted to die in peace, without Andrew around to hurt me some more.

"You don't look so great."

Probably had a lot to do with the fact I'd tried to kill myself. Didn't he feel any regret? It was all his fault...

He sat down in the chair Mum had abandoned earlier. He rested his hands on his stomach, spread his legs, gaze firmly locked on me.

I didn't want to meet his gaze. I couldn't stand to look and see the cold, hard truth: he didn't care. He didn't care at all about me, except for what I did for him. All that mattered for him was him. No one else were as important as his happiness, his needs. Even if he had to ruin someone's life, as long as he got what he needed, he didn't give a damn.

What had made him like this? I'd asked myself that hundreds—maybe even thousands—of times throughout the years. Something must've happened to him when he was younger to make him into the monster he was now… He couldn't have simply been born like this, could he? Like the sick, sadistic, cruel, paedophilic pervert that he was?

Maybe what he'd been doing to me had been happening to him when he was young? I'd never liked that possible explanation. I didn't want to think for even a second that having experienced what I did could make a person do the exact same thing to someone else. A ruined life ruins another one, and so the circle continues.

I would never do to anyone else what had happened to me. No one should have to live in fear their whole childhood, of being used in ways a child should never be used, of hurting themselves just to dull the emotional pain, where the only way out was suicide.

"Are you going to keep giving me the silent treatment?" His voice washed over me, cool, cold, non-caring. There was no emotion in it. I didn't matter, I wasn't even worth a single *emotion*. "Crying again, are we?"

I didn't even realise I was until he commented on it. All that mattered to me— was the monster he was. Even if he had some sad, tragic backstory, it would never make me sympathise with him. Not ever. Not after everything he'd done to me, after all these years...

"What do you want?" The words came out shaky.

"You're in hospital. I'm here to visit, as is the rest of your family."

Hardly. Only Mum and Grandma. The rest of them were back in Bristol.

"Oh, they're all here." He leant forward, eyes narrowing. "They all came rushing down to be with you once your mum told them what happened." His hand gripped my wrist and I tried to jerk away because it hurt, it was just stitched up, but he only tightened his grip. "Don't you dare tell them anything. I swear—"

I didn't get to know what he'd swear, because he broke off as the door opened. All I could do was stare at him in terror, tears streaming because he was hurting me. And it was too late! I'd already told. I'd told Mum. And he'd find out… and then he'd punish me. He'd punish me so bad. And I couldn't take it, I just couldn't. Not him, not again, not ever.

As soon as I got out of here, I was going to die. I was going to succeed at it. There was no other choice!

CHAPTER 14

Waking up drenched in sweat and with a heart beating a mile a minute wasn't exactly an uncommon thing. In fact, it was quite common. But it was usually from worse memories than the one I'd been dreaming about. Memories where he'd hurt me properly. Now he'd just been sitting there, staring at me, intimidating me. He did that so well. Always had.

Even though I was drenched in sweat, I was cold. So cold I shook, teeth chattering. My tee and joggers clung to me, the duvet tangled in my legs.

"Hey… Come on." Damian was at my side, arm sliding around my waist, boosting me up. I followed him blindly, still seeing those eyes flash before my mind. All I heard was the sound of my teeth chattering together.

"He d-didn't even d-do anything."

"What?" We were out of the bedroom, in the even colder hallway, then Damian led me into the warm bathroom.

"It was the hospital. He didn't do anything to me there... but he was just *sitting* there. Staring at me. Being all intimidating. Telling me I'd regret it if I told anyone—" Why couldn't those cold eyes go away, it was like they were burned onto my retinas.

"Come on, get those clothes off."

I did as he directed, still not able to get rid of the look in those *eyes*. It was the last time he'd been that close to me, and even if he hadn't hurt me, it'd been terrifying.

The hot water hit me in the face, and it shocked me enough to snap out of what had still kept me locked in the terror of the nightmare.

"It's okay." Damian's hands slid over my shoulder-blades, caressing and kneading slightly as the hot water washed down over me.

I bent my head under the spray. It felt so good to have the hot water beating down, washing away the sweat and the terror along with it.

"It's all okay. It's just me here. Me and you."

There was a squirt of a bottle, then his hands were on my skin again, rubbing soap over me.

That was the moment I realised he was actually *in* the shower with me. I glanced over my shoulder to see his bare torso, just to see if it was true. We hardly ever showered together. I could count on my hands the times I'd seen him naked in the last three years.

But even if we didn't get naked and jump into bed, our relationship was just as strong as Silver and Kian's—and they took every opportunity to both get naked *and* jump into bed for some fun together.

I turned abruptly, then slowly leaned in to rest my cheek against his. "I'm so lucky."

"Why?" His hands kept rubbing, slowly sliding down to my waist, and then to rub soap over my hips.

"Because I've got you. You've been here for me, no matter what a mess I've been."

"I think I'm lucky to have you."

I couldn't help the derisive snort that left me. "Yeah, because I'm such a great catch."

"You're the only catch I've ever been interested in catching." A laugh escaped him as he belatedly realised the cheesiness of that sentence.

But it was enough. It had me laughing along with him. It felt so good to laugh again, it felt like it was a lifetime ago since I'd done it last.

He gave up trying to wash me and instead wrapped his arms around me in a hug. I pulled my head back slightly so I could look at him, and the laughter died in my throat as his gaze met mine.

I was still so in love with him. It washed over me in that moment, like a calming blanket. It bolstered, it strengthened, and my chest tightened almost painfully good at it.

I kissed him. Or he kissed me. It didn't matter which of us took the initiative. All that mattered was that we were kissing and that it was good and great and so long-awaited. When was the last time we'd properly kissed? I couldn't even remember it.

Kissing wasn't sexual for him, and it really wasn't for me either. Not to say I didn't feel it further down, but kissing was more a comfort. It was intimacy, the most intimate our bodies would ever be. And yes, a great comfort. To know that he, who hadn't even liked kissing in the beginning, now enjoyed it as much as I did... it was exhilarating.

Is it possible to love someone so much? He was everything to me. As much as I hated Andrew, I loved Damian just as much. But sometimes, the hatred and the terrors overwhelmed the love and I did stupid stuff. Like trying to kill myself.

I wanted to be with Damian more than anything else. But the impulsiveness... it could be fatal, especially when I was so far down the black hole I couldn't even see a glimpse of light in the far distance. When everything was so bad, so all-consuming bad, all that mattered was to make it stop.

He could make it stop, what we had together could make it stop, but he wasn't always there. I couldn't expect him to be. But he was here now and the horrid memories fell away as we pressed together, as we kept kissing. The water still washed down on us, but it didn't matter. All that mattered was him, this, *us*.

When we were like this, nothing else could penetrate our own little bubble. It was only us, and it was good, so wonderful, and I never wanted the bubble to burst. It always did, whenever the spell broke, but for the time we spent like this, it was definitely worth it.

"Put whatever you want in the trolley, Josh."

Claire smiled at me as she breezed through the aisles. She'd dragged me to the supermarket with her, saying that I couldn't stay cooped up in the house all day, that I needed to get out. I agreed—so I went with.

It was safe going out with someone else. Andrew

would never do anything to me when other people were around. Still, I was wary of going out in public alone. Someone had to come with me, someone I knew.

Today it was Claire and I.

Ray was back home preparing dinner till we came back, with help from Matilda. Matt was… I didn't know what Matt was. Probably cooped up in his room. He was more moody than I was nowadays.

"Don't you want anything?" Claire stared into the trolley. It only contained items she herself had put there.

I shrugged. I didn't have much of an appetite lately, but I ate whatever they made for dinner. Since they were so kind and let me stay with them, it was the least I could do. But I didn't want her to pay for anything else on my behalf.

"Come on." She nudged me. "What about crisps? What do you like? We're having a film night this weekend and everyone likes different kinds of snacks."

I looked over the assortment, and grabbed a bag of ready salted crisps. "This one, maybe."

"Great." She took it from me and put it in the trolley. Then she grabbed several other bags of crisps as well.

I smiled slightly and pushed the trolley after her

as she continued along the aisle. Claire was so happy, so kind, so down-to-earth. *I wish I could be like that.*

"Josh, could you grab me some toilet paper over there?" Claire motioned to the other side of the aisle.

I left the trolley with her, where she was perusing women's toiletries, and headed back to the paper section. I didn't know what brand she preferred, and she hadn't said, so I took one that wasn't too expensive.

As I turned to head back to her, someone walked right into me. Our shoulders crashed together and I staggered back. *A man, taller than me, blond hair—*

I couldn't breathe.

"Hey, sorry, mate." Blue eyes looked at me through black-rimmed glasses, before the man hurried on his way.

I let out the breath I'd been holding, relief flooding me. *It wasn't Andrew.*

"Josh?" Claire called, a worried tinge to her voice.

I clutched the toilet paper to my chest and ambled back over to the trolley. "I'm sorry."

Her eyebrows drew together in a frown. "Did he hurt you? Your arm?"

My arm? *Oh yeah, the stitches.* "No, I was just surprised, that's all." I didn't want to admit out loud I'd thought for a moment he was Andrew. They'd all made it perfectly clear he wasn't out there to get me, that there wasn't anyone out there watching. That it was my paranoia, set off by my borderline personality.

But it's not. It isn't.

He is *out there.*

Maybe he wasn't here in the shop. But he *had* been watching me when I sat on the stairs, keeping an eye on Storm. And he had been stalking me. I knew it. I wasn't wrong. *I can't be wrong.*

They all said I was wrong—so I had to be right? But I couldn't shake it. And I had no idea if this conviction of mine he was out to get me really was founded in reality, or if it truly was paranoia because of my diagnosis. I'd never had paranoia about anything before, not like this.

I hate this. I hate myself. Hate my mind.

I hate being borderline.

I hated not being able to trust myself.

FIVE YEARS AGO

J wasn't aware he'd stopped talking because of the door opening before I heard voices.

"Step away from the bed, sir."

My head turned slowly to find not just one, but two uniformed officers. *What?* What was going on?

Andrew rose. "What's going on?" *Like he read my mind.*

Voices drowned out. All I could see, all I could register, was how there was a pair of handcuffs out in the open all of a sudden. A pair of handcuffs that wasn't used on me, but on *him*.

He threw me a look, a furious one that never boded well for me... but now he was in *handcuffs*.

Two officers were there to take him away. They would, wouldn't they? They had to! Lock him up, lock him away, far, far away from me.

My ears were ringing. Andrew's lips were moving but I didn't hear what he was saying. My gaze zeroed in on his lips, on their movement, but no sound reached me. Nothing but the ringing and the sound of my own heart beating wildly.

He didn't fight them. He walked out calm as ever.

One moment he was there, the next he was gone. Led out, in handcuffs, arrested.

Joshua…

Joshua?

Joshua!

I blinked, dazed.

"Joshua?"

It was Mum. She was there, next to my bed.

She took a step closer, then stopped. She put her hands behind her back, looked away.

I swallowed the lump that was stuck in my throat. "You b-believe me?"

She still didn't look at me, but her nod was terse. "Of course I do."

Of course… There was no of course. I'd always believed she wouldn't. And here she was, telling me that of course she did. How was I supposed to know that she'd believe me? She'd always been too busy to bother with me. She'd left me in Andrew's care while her career soared.

"Where's Grandma?" It was weird that she wasn't here by my side.

"Still at home. I haven't told her yet."

The lump was back, so big I couldn't even swallow it. "W-why?" Did she want me to keep this quiet? Didn't she want anyone else to know? But she'd had Andrew arrested... of course the rest of the family would find out.

She sank onto the chair next to my bed. Her head turned to face me, green eyes staring at me. I couldn't face that stare, so I turned my head away.

"I'm so sorry."

I tilted my head in her direction. "What're you sorry for?"

"For not seeing the signs." She turned her head away so I couldn't look at her anymore. "I should've seen the signs of what was going on, of what he was doing to you."

"He was very careful not to let you know." My lap had become very interesting all of a sudden.

"I still should've seen them. I should've seen the signs better than anyone." Her hands were balled into fists, gripping the fabric of her trousers in-between them.

Those words held meaning, I could feel it. "What do you mean?" My voice shook.

She hesitated with her answer, and I could see her internal struggle due to the rapid changes in her expression. Even in profile they were obvious.

"I've never told anyone this before, and now I'm sitting here, telling you. I know I haven't been a good mum to you, that I've left you to your own devices—to him—and that I've been largely absent. I am so sorry about that. I never meant to be absent from your life, to not even know you. For sixteen years I ignored my own son, leaving him in the single care of my husband while I focused on my career. It's no excuse though to ignore you, it really isn't. I am so ashamed, and all I can do is tell you how sorry I am and how much I want to make it up to you. If that's even possible at this point."

I heard what she was saying, every word of it, but my mind had stuck on her first sentence and I couldn't let it go. "What'd you mean? What've you never told anyone?" My voice still shook, but it also demanded answers. I needed to know.

She glanced up at me, but when our eyes met, she quickly turned away again. "I should've seen the signs because—" She took a shaky breath. "Because I've been exactly where you are, Joshua."

My eyes widened. "W-what?"

"I've been a victim of sexual abuse too." She closed her eyes as if she was in pain. She probably was. I knew better than anyone just how much the inside could hurt. I bet talking about it had her remembering all over again and I shuddered at the thought.

I couldn't take my eyes off her. I was frozen in place. "You? But— Who? Who did that to you?"

She pressed her lips together into a small line. "My father." It came out as a bitter snarl, like the word was the worst of curses. "For four very long years he did things to me. Then he was diagnosed with cancer and died. Months of pain were what he got, because the cancer had already spread and there was nothing they could do. I didn't feel sorry for him. I was happy he was suffering. Karma had come back and properly bitch-slapped him in the face. He got what he deserved, and when he died, I was happy then too. I would never have to see his face again, I would never have him crawling into my bed."

My throat had gone dry. "How old were you?"

"From I was ten till I was fourteen."

Four years of violation. It was nothing to my ten, but it was still four years too much. At least Andrew wasn't related to me by blood. He was just my stepfather. She'd been violated by her very own dad, the man whose genes she shared.

"Does Grandma know?"

She looked back at me, eyes a dark green. "No. And she never will. Promise me you'll never tell her, Joshua. You're the only one I've ever told. Not even Abbi—my own sister—knows what a bastard of a father we had. Knowing this would destroy Mum and she doesn't deserve that."

"I won't tell." I understood her, because I hadn't wanted anyone to know about my circumstances either. But once I'd woken up and had been told I would be fine, that I would have no damage from the pills and that I would be able to go back home ... I'd lost it. I couldn't go back home when he would be there.

And Mum had been there. She'd listened, with tears trickling, and now I finally got to hear her story.

She turned to me again. "It saddens me that I've shut you out so completely you didn't feel like you could ever come to me with this. I never had time—I didn't care enough—to get to know you properly, so I never even imagined anything was wrong. I'm so sorry, Joshua." The tears were overflowing now, trickling slowly down her cheeks.

"It's okay. I didn't want you to know. I didn't

want anyone to know." I was so ashamed and humiliated. Used as my own stepfather's blow-up doll and punching bag for ten years, and then failing at committing suicide when I'd finally had enough. When I couldn't take it anymore.

CHAPTER 15

"*H*ow are you finding the locks around here, Josh?"

Ray strode into the kitchen, his tone teasing as he glanced over at me.

I flushed, embarrassed. "They seem to work just fine." I couldn't believe I'd freaked out so much about two locks as to ring him at work—and had him come over to check them out.

"Good." He clapped me on the back, good-naturedly. He headed over to the refrigerator where he poured himself a glass of milk, then sat down across from me on the table. "What are you up to?"

"I'm trying to write. A book," I clarified, before he could ask. My laptop was open in front of me, but the document glared white at me as it always did. I had managed a chapter since I'd come to stay with them, but starting a new one was as difficult as the previous one had been.

"Oh yeah?" His eyebrows rose. "What do you write about?"

I shrugged awkwardly, embarrassed for a whole other reason now. "Stuff. Romance." It was supposed to be a love story, sort of based on Damian and I. I didn't want it to be entirely autobiographical, but it seemed to turn out that way anyway. I hadn't wanted anyone borderline in the book, at all, but *that* had happened anyway. *That's the character based on me, then*. The main character, the character from whose point of view the entire story was told.

"Romance novels, huh? Didn't know you liked those." He wriggled his eyebrows now. "Claire does. You'll have to let her read it when you're done."

I managed a small smile, but it was tinged with self-consciousness. "Maybe. Right now I'm not sure I even like it myself. Maybe I won't finish it." I wanted to though. It was like I needed to get the words down.

It was almost like back when I used to write journals. I *had* to do it. I'd stopped with my journals now, and it had turned into this massive need to write fiction instead. Fiction based on real life, because my demons would never leave me and I had to channel them somewhere.

"Maybe you'll be an author, huh?" Ray said, emptying his glass. "That would be nice for you, wouldn't it? Work your own hours, and from home, too."

He had a point there. I didn't think I ever could get a proper job. Not one that involved other people, or stress, or… anything really. I couldn't deal with life, all the ups and downs it brought. I could hardly deal with my own head.

"Yeah, it would be," I agreed quietly, but my mind whirled.

Maybe he was onto something. I wasn't exactly getting any better, and I was headed straight for disability. If Mum hadn't come from money, I probably would've been on disability by now. And I needed to do *something*. I couldn't walk around at home all day, everyday.

Writing was an outlet. It let me get my thoughts and feelings out, down on paper—or the screen anyway. Journaling had helped me through my childhood. Clearly it was something that was good for me.

"If you ever do finish it, maybe you'll let me read it too." Ray's voice broke me out of my thoughts.

I smiled, albeit weakly. Letting anyone read something I'd written left me all kinds of nervous. But that they wanted to read it was nice to know. "Yeah, maybe."

Ray chuckled. "Or not, if it makes you uncomfortable. Has Damian read anything you've written?"

I shook my head. "No." I'd written some short stuff, short stories, but I hadn't even so much as told him about them. They were my secret escape. Maybe someday I'd let him read them, let other people read them too, but today wasn't that day.

"I've got to start dinner." Ray pushed away from the table and stood. "I promised Claire I would today. She had to stay an hour longer at work."

"Can I help?" I asked, tired of looking at the blank document.

"You can peel the potatoes."

I shut my laptop, feeling somewhat relieved I didn't have to sit there and worry about how to start the next chapter. It also felt good that I could help, even something as trivial as peeling potatoes for dinner.

SPENDING time at Ray and Claire's home was rather relaxing. They didn't live in the middle of London with all the people and traffic and the noise that brought with it. They had a big house, a big garden, quiet neighbours around the street.

I needed the quiet, the relaxing, the comfortable atmosphere of a happy family. Ray and Claire were as nice and warm as ever, Matilda was mostly busy with her own things outside the house, and though Matt was taciturn he at least seemed more happy now the puppy was around.

Storm definitely lifted my moods as well, and I frequently fell into one or the other. Damian was at school every day, Ray and Claire at work, Matilda and Matt at school, and I was home with the puppy and my laptop and my thoughts.

I had to figure out what I wanted to do with my life. I couldn't start and quit university anymore. I had to figure out one thing I could stick to—without the expectations and the stress landing me in hospital again.

As I sat there, poring over different websites and in the process of answering a questionnaire that would apparently tell me what kind of career I would be best suited for, my phone rang.

The screen showed Kian's name and I answered immediately. "Hi."

"Hi! How are you feeling?"

"Good." For once, that was true. It could all

change in a second, I was more than aware of that, but for now… for now I felt good.

"That's good, Josh. Look, I just rang to ask if you wanted to join us at the pub later tonight? Have something to eat, a few pints, you know."

Now that sounded good! It'd been a while since I'd had some quality time with friends. "Who's us?"

"Well, for now it's just me and Silver. But if you come, so will Damian. And if you're up for more company, there's no reason there should just be the four of us."

Storm shifted at my feet, a heavy sigh leaving her. Fondness washed over me as I gazed down at her.

"That sounds great, Kian." It did. I felt ready to go out, to face the world. Maybe even move back home. "Text me the place and time and I'll be there."

"Awesome! Talk to you later."

I put my phone down next to my computer and gazed at it. I should text Damian, tell him the plan. I could invite Cooper, perhaps… or not. He and Damian were no fan of each other. Maybe Leslie and Spencer, old co-workers of Damian who'd also worked at Harriet's Café. They were more my friends than his, which was a bit weird, considering he'd worked with them long before he ever met me. But then Damian wasn't the most sociable of blokes. He was happy with just Silver.

I jumped in my seat as a door slammed.

Was anyone supposed to come home now? I glanced at the clock on my laptop. It was too early.

Storm had woken up at my feet and both her ears were standing right up in alert.

I got off my chair and inched over to the doorway. I had a bad feeling. A really bad one. I glanced one way, towards the hallway. That door was closed, there was no shoes or jackets or rucksacks to witness another presence in the house.

The other way... My heart literally skipped a beat. The veranda door was open. Not wide open, but lolling a bit, exactly as if it'd been slammed open and hadn't managed to slide back closed afterwards.

No one used the veranda door, unless they were in the house and actually heading out to the veranda. No one entered the house that way. What was the point? The veranda was round the back of the house.

I hurried over to it, looked outside. No one there. Which meant... someone was in the house. Something cold slithered down my back, the hairs at the back of my neck rose.

Something moved. I could see it in the glass of the door. I stood frozen—until someone grabbed the back of my neck and shoved me forward, slamming my forehead against the glass.

I didn't even need to turn around, or hear his

voice, to know who it was. I didn't need any of that for the terror to spread through me. But he did speak, and it was in the same calm, cold tone I heard almost every time I was asleep.

"Hello, Joshua."

TWO YEARS AND EIGHT
MONTHS AGO

The witness box loomed in front of me. I had to go up there, I had to tell them everything. Every single little thing he'd ever done to me—or what I could remember, anyway.

My journals weren't enough. I had to stand up there, in front of everyone, and tell my story. Like the journals didn't tell enough. Why did they have to hear me say it? They'd taken all the journals in as evidence… Why couldn't that be enough?

He was sitting there. Behind glass, yes, but fully visible.

I had to face him. Again.

I hadn't faced him since that day in my hospital room, when he'd been arrested. Now here I was, about to give evidence. And he was right there.

His eyes were on me.

Mine were on the witness box. Where I had to walk to. Where I had to stand. Where I had to not gloss over it like I'd done to Mum in my hospital room, but to go into every single detail I could remember. And I had to do it in front of all these strangers.

And worst of all… in front of him.

CHAPTER 16

*H*is hand, his big, cold hand, clamped around the back of my neck. My forehead hurt from where he'd slammed me against the glass.

I couldn't do anything, couldn't say anything. Frozen in terror, that's what I was. His hands were on me for the first time since I was fifteen. It brought it all back more clearly than any nightmare ever could. It overwhelmed me.

"Lucky me, got you all alone."

Alone… No one was here. They were all at work, at school… I was all alone with *him*. Because I didn't have anything worthwhile to fill my days with, I had to spend them alone, when I knew *he* was on the loose and *following* me.

How stupid could I be?

I didn't realise what he was doing until my knees connected painfully with the floor. I barely caught myself with my hands right before my nose would've made a very forceful introduction to the floor.

I scrambled away. Instant relief flooded me when he didn't grab my hips and force me back down. I dared a look over my shoulder as I pushed myself up.

He was standing there, staring at me, hands hanging at his sides. Eyes as cold as ever. They hadn't changed. He hadn't changed. Same bloody bastard he'd always been. And once again, I was at his mercy.

"What do you want?" My voice didn't sound like me.

His eyes narrowed. "You ruined me." He lunged for me, and I was too slow— His hand locked around the back of my neck and he forced me face-down on the floor. "People in prison aren't too fond of those who've been with children."

Had someone given him a taste of what it'd been like to be me? Or maybe they'd just beat the shit out of him. Whatever it was, I hoped it had hurt. I hoped it had hurt *good*. But it hadn't hurt good enough, or permanently enough, because here he was. And here

I was, just as helpless as I'd always been. At his mercy, as I'd been for such a long time.

Whatever he wanted to do to me, he could. He'd always been able to. I wasn't strong enough to fight him. I never had been.

Claws clicked on the floor. Looking up, I saw Storm standing there, head cocked to one side as she took us in.

Go away. I wanted to shout it at her, but my throat didn't work. I didn't want her harmed. Let Andrew do whatever he wanted to me—I'd taken it before, I could take it again—but let *her* be. She was just a puppy. Defenseless…

"You have no idea—" Andrew was breathing heavily, I could feel his chest rising and falling against my shoulder, I could feel his breath on my temple. "No bloody idea what it was like."

I had an idea. I would've preferred prison to the ten years with him, if I could've chosen. Never would I choose him.

"What am I going to do now, huh? Branded an abuser, a paedophile. You *ruined* me."

It was so unfair. "You r-ruined me." I didn't know I'd dared speak until I heard myself say it and felt the tightening of his hand. Tears leaked from beneath the eyelids I'd just closed.

"Ruined *you*?" He was enraged now. "You've got

a life, no convictions to tie you down, you've got a boyfriend, a family! And me? I've got *nothing*."

"Sh-should've th-thought of th-that—"

He slammed my head against the floor before I could finish. I cried out, pain spreading through my head. I swear I saw stars for a moment.

Painful sobs escaped me. "P-please…" I didn't know what I was begging for. I'd begged him so many times—for the pain to stop, for him to stop, for him to simply finish, for him to never come into my room, for him to quickly get out of my room—and now… I just wanted it to be over with.

He let go of me. I lay stunned for a second, then crawled forward.

Storm was still standing there, head now tilting to the other side. "Go!" My hand hit her as I threw it out towards her, and she scrambled back, turning a wounded look my way. "Go away." Tears leaked again from that look. I didn't want to hurt her, but I *had*. I couldn't take those big, wounded eyes staring at me. "Please go!"

"You care more for a dog than yourself?"

Of course I did. I'd experienced so much, so much bad, but I didn't want her to experience that. She had to leave, she didn't have to see this, whatever it was he wanted to do to me.

He grabbed me, threw me forwards. We were in

the kitchen now, and I hit the edge of the counter before I collapsed on the floor.

"D-don't…" I pushed up, hoping to slip around the kitchen table or grab a knife or *anything*… but his hand locked around my neck again.

The edge of the table came flying towards me… and blackness played before my eyes as it hit.

I did crumple on the floor then. Something warm ran down the side of my face. It wasn't tears. It must be blood. It all *hurt*…

"Good riddance, Joshua."

Steps. Going away.

I must've faded in and out, because I didn't hear a door. The next thing I heard was a car revving, and then nothing until there was an ear-splitting crash.

I hope he wrapped that car of his around a lamp post. I hope it wraps around him and crushes him.

The pain had stopped… I didn't feel anything.

And then it all went black.

*T*he verdict.

It was ready, it was being read.

My hands were balled into fists, so tight I was losing blood flow. But it didn't matter. Nothing mattered but the verdict.

The foreperson answered a question. Yes, the verdict was ready. No, it was not unanimous.

Not unanimous? Someone didn't agree? But what didn't they agree with? That Andrew was guilty? Did someone think I was lying?

I wasn't. How could I make something as awful as this up? How could someone choose not to believe with all the evidence? My journals... Did they think a ten-year-old kid would make up what was depicted in one of the earliest journals?

I held my breath, sitting as quietly as I could, scared to hear the verdict, scared I'd miss it.

The foreperson parted her lips… I watched them, transfixed.

"We find the defendant…"

Oh god. Please, please, please. End this. Don't let him walk off now, not after everything.

"Guilty."

PART III
DEATH

noun.
the act of dying; the end of life; the total and
permanent cessation of all the vital functions of an
organism.

CHAPTER 17

I heard the *beeping* first.

Then sniffling.

My eyelids fought me, but I managed to force them open in a slit. All I saw was the ceiling. My neck fought me next, but I did manage to turn it slightly. And now I did see.

I saw Damian.

And he was crying.

He was sitting in a chair, like he'd done the last time I'd woken up in hospital, but this time he looked starkly different. He'd been worried, scared then too, but now... He looked *wounded*. He was hunched over, temple resting against the back of his hand, which again rested against the wall.

His eyes... they were red-rimmed and sore. I'd

seen Damian worried, I'd seen him panicked, I'd seen him with tears *in* his eyes, but this... this was so much more. This was *grief*.

Andrew!

My whole body shuddered at the name, at what now flashed before me inside my mind. A shaking breath left me—and that brought Damian's attention to me.

"Josh!" He stood so quick from the chair that for a second it was on the verge of tilting over.

I wanted to speak, to say his name, but the memories consumed me. The last few minutes of my *life*—or so it had seemed. Why wasn't I dead? He'd wanted me dead. Why hadn't he done the job properly?

"An-Andrew—"

Damian's face, which had turned from grief to relief, now clouded over. "Back in prison. Where he belongs."

Still alive. But back behind bars. It was something, at least. Though I really had hoped he rot.

There were so much else I wanted to ask. My throat worked, but no words came out.

"Rest, Josh." He stroked my cheek, forehead, other cheek. "Rest up."

His voice was deceptively calm and collected, but his eyes... they weren't. They told a whole other story. A really bad story.

I hoped he hadn't been the one to find me. I had no idea what kind of state I'd been in, last I remember was my head connecting against the table. *Please don't let him be the one who found me*.

"Please, Josh. Go to sleep. You need to rest." He was begging me now.

I did as he pleaded. It didn't even require anything from me—I easily slipped back into sleep. It was like I drifted, but awake to asleep, and then back again to reality once in a while.

I could've been drifting in and out for mere minutes or hours, I had no idea. All I knew was my head was spinning from it whenever I did wake. I heard voices but couldn't make them out, because I drifted back into darkness before anything registered.

But now… now I didn't fall back asleep. I kept my eyes closed, because it was so comfortable, but I could hear whispered voices in the room.

"You need to go home, Damian." It was Mum.

"I can't leave him."

"You've been here *days*. You haven't gone home, haven't showered, haven't slept, haven't relaxed—"

"How can I possibly relax?" It came out forceful. I'd never heard Damian be forceful with my mum before. Not with anyone, really.

Silence. "I know you're worried. I know you're

afraid. We all are. But he woke up, Damian. He'll come through this." Mum sounded so sure.

"Will he?" Damian wasn't though. He sounded like me now: eternal pessimist. "When he wakes up properly, when he's starting to ask questions— I have to *tell* him. You really think he'll be okay once he knows?"

Mum didn't answer. Maybe she nodded—or shook her head. Likely the latter. When was I ever okay? Whatever it was that had happened… It must be bad.

I thought back. Andrew had slammed my head against the table. I'd fallen to the floor.

"Good riddance, Joshua." It was like he was standing next to me, that's how well his voice rang in my ear.

But he'd walked away. He'd left me there on the floor. Left me to die. I'd heard him rev his car… and I'd heard a crash. I'd hoped he died. He was alive though. Alive and well, in prison once again. So what could be so bad?

My blood ran cold. Had he come back for me again? Had he done something to me whilst I'd been unconscious? Whilst I'd been lying there in my own blood, slowly dying? Had he come back to have his way with me once again?

My chest hurt, my breath heaved painfully.

There was a sudden commotion around me, but nothing could penetrate my own terror and not being able to breathe, at not being able to know what had been done to me.

And then all went dark again.

*T*he rain fit perfectly with me right now.

My eyes burned from all the tears they'd shed. That they were still shedding. I couldn't stop crying.

I couldn't keep walking either. I collapsed against a tree trunk and sunk onto the wet grass squishing under my trainers.

I didn't care what I looked like—though I must look quite pathetic. It was no one's business. Not that anyone would know I was crying—thanks to the rain.

Good thing about people was they were so easy. Someone young like me, curled up on the ground, in tears, in nothing but jeans and a thin shirt, would make everyone steer away from me. I could be homeless or a druggie or anything. It wasn't something anyone wanted to have anything to do with.

Eight bloody years.

Not enough. Not enough by a long shot.

He'd ruined ten years for me—from the abuse itself. Maybe even longer, because I had absolutely no idea when it had actually started. Not to mention the two years since he'd been arrested and removed from my life… he'd ruined me, and thus he'd ruined those two years too. Finally free from him, but I was just as much a mess as I'd been when he'd still been in my life.

So eight years… Not nearly enough.

Someone was walking close to me, over the grass. I heard the squishy sounds. Leave me alone. Leave me alone. Please, just leave me alone. I didn't want to deal with anyone, not in any kind of way.

"If you stay like this you'll get sick."

The voice gave me a start. It wasn't said in the most friendliest of tones, but it didn't sound like he was being mean either, like he was looking at me. Though he was, standing up and all.

He sounded young too. Not like the old geezers that were out on the prowl for young flesh.

I wiped my face. Looked up.

And I was gone.

It wasn't love at first sight, I didn't even have

such emotion in me, but… he was my age, he was handsome, and he seemed more worried than busy out looking to stem his own pleasures.

"I c-can't go h-home." My teeth chattered. I hadn't even known I was cold until that minute. My emotions were intense like that, they drowned out everything else. When they spiked anyway, not when I was in the normal range of it. But then, when was I ever in a normal range?

He wanted to know why I couldn't go home, I stood fast by the fact I couldn't. I could, of course, no one would stop me. They'd welcome me. They were worrying now, I knew it. But I couldn't stomach it, couldn't stomach facing all of them, not now… so I couldn't go home.

"Don't you have any friends you can go to?"

I stared hard at the wet grass. "No. I don't have any friends." No one wanted to be mates with me. I'd never been open to mates either, had always had too much with my own shit. Still had too much with my own shit. Likely always would, at this point.

"You can't stay out here. You'll get pneumonia. I guess you could—" He stopped himself. I could hear him swallow, as if he was nervous. "You could come with me. I live right across the street."

Now that was more like I'd expected. I looked up at him, taking him in again. It really wouldn't be a chore. And I'd have someplace dry and warm—hopefully anyway—to stay for the nights. It would be better than going home right now, even if I had to put out. "You sure?"

"Yeah." He didn't seem entirely sure though. Maybe he was shy. "Yeah, come on."

I went.

CHAPTER 18

I was alone. My room was eerily quiet, despite the beeping of one of those machines still hooked up to me. Did they think I was going to fall back into unconsciousness? Or was it standard procedure? Likely the latter. I should know, considering all the time I'd spent in hospital in my life. Still. The *beeping* was annoying.

Where were everyone? Last time I'd been in hospital—by my own doing, none the less, whereas this time was certainly not my fault—someone had been with me at all times possible.

Now I was alone.

Completely, utterly alone.

I was more lucid now than I'd been back then. I was able to speak and I wanted to ask questions. I had to *know*. I couldn't stand lying here without any idea what had happened after I'd passed out. What he'd done to me.

But that crash…

My eyes fell shut as I tried to remember. I'd been fading, but I had definitely heard a crash. What had that been all about? Gad, he hadn't crashed his bloody car into the house, had he?

I jerked forwards, a little too quick for my head's liking, as I now groaned in pain. After tentatively feeling the bandage that was wrapped around it, making sure it was in place, I lay back against my pillow.

He can't have ruined the house. Ray and Claire loved their house, it was their dream home. They spent so much time and energy and money on upkeep, so that they had a home they could live in for the rest of their lives.

Not knowing what had happened was killing me. I *had* to know. What had he *done* to me? Besides making sure my head connected against the table and then, presumably anyway, leaving me to die.

A doctor appeared in the doorway. Here was a chance of finally getting some answers.

"What happened to me? Besides the head injury—"

He regarded me in silence for a long moment. "There was just the head trauma."

"But—" That didn't make any sense. "He didn't do anything to me? Anything else?"

"The head trauma was quite severe. You were in a coma for four days."

Coma? For four *days?* I blinked. No wonder Damian had looked wrecked. No wonder he and Mum had been whispering about not telling me something. It was *this. Coma.*

I lay quietly as he checked me over, retreating into my own mind which flashed the word *coma* in bright neon letters so it was impossible to ignore. *In a coma.* I hadn't even been in a coma when I'd overdosed on my stupid pills... No wonder Damian had been crying when I first woke up.

The doctor left. Time ticked by. I was alone. No one *came.* Where were they? Had they all given up on me? *But this wasn't my fault. I can't be held liable for this.*

"Hey, Josh."

I startled.

Silver and Kian were there, both peering down at me in worry.

"Oh, hey." I couldn't hide my disappointment.

"Not who you wanted to see, were we?" Silver's lips hitched up, barely, on one side.

"Damian hasn't been here today." Okay, that was a bit unfair. It wasn't long since I'd woken up, after all, and I didn't know which day it was. Was this the same day as I'd first woken, as when I'd overheard Damian and Mum? Or was this another day entirely? I had no idea. It was disorienting.

"He'll be back. He had something to do."

His voice had turned… weird. "What did he have to do?"

"He'll tell you when he gets here, I reckon."

It was my turn to peer up at him. Something was going on. Something was wrong. I felt it in my whole body.

"I'm so happy you're okay." Kian bent down to hug me—gingerly so, as I must have looked pretty fragile in a hospital bed and with my head in bandages. He also pressed a chaste kiss to my cheek, which was nice.

"Four days in a coma." I couldn't stop thinking about it. Who would after waking up and hearing that? "The doctor said so."

They both nodded gravely. Silver was the one to speak, "He's right. Four days. We've been worried."

What must he have gone through for four days? And Mum too… Tears were pressing. *Again*. Was I ever going to stop crying? It was getting tiresome—

and if it was getting tiresome for me, it definitely had to be so for everyone else.

"I wish he'd come see me."

"He's been here nearly twenty-four seven since you were admitted."

Speaking of which… "Who found me? In the house— and the dog! Is Storm okay?"

"The dog's fine." Silver exchanged a look with Kian, but quickly turned his attention back to me. Kian stared at the floor, biting his lower lip. Why were they acting so *weird*? "She got scared away, if even that. I'm not sure Storm even understands what happened, but at least she wasn't hurt."

"They can be quite smart." She was just a puppy though. "So who found me?" I hoped it wasn't Damian. Or Mum. She'd found me unconscious more than enough already. I hoped it wasn't Ray or Claire or Matilda or Matt either… I hoped it was a stranger, but that was too much to hope for. Why would a stranger come into the house when no one else were home?

"It was Matt."

No. Matt had enough as it was, what with him possibly cutting himself. Possibly being depressed. Finding me unconscious on the floor, likely with blood on and around me, was not going to be a help for his mental condition. If indeed there was a condition, which I couldn't be entirely sure of. It could just be teenaged brooding.

They exchanged glances again. They were keeping something back from me. Something I wasn't supposed to know.

I didn't have the energy or the will to demand answers. *Matt* had found me. It would've been better if it was anyone else—well, not Matilda either, but she seemed in better mental health than Matt, so...

The sound of steps alerted me to presence of other people outside my room. I heard heels clacking against the floor— and then Mum breezed into the room, quickly followed by Damian. Mum was stony-faced. Damian looked miserable.

"Hey." I glanced anxiously between them. "I'm fine. Really." They didn't have to look like that. It might've been bad, but it wasn't anymore. Unless the doctor had shared something with them he hadn't told me?

At my side, I caught Kian grabbing a hold of Silver's hand. "Let's leave them alone."

Silver nodded, then reached out to pat my shoulder. "See you later, Josh."

The four of them exchanged silenced nods as Silver and Kian left and Damian and Mum took their places next to my bed. Mum took the chair, Damian perched at edge of my bed.

"What's wrong?" There had to be something. "What's wrong with me? The doctor said it was only the head injury— I feel fine."

"You'll be fine, Joshua." Mum glanced up at Damian, who was resolutely staring down at the floor.

If I would be fine, it wasn't me making them look like this. I fumbled for Damian's hand. Squeezed it once I found it. "What's the matter? Damian…"

His Adam's apple moved as he swallowed heavily.

"Is it Matt?" He'd found me. Perhaps it had been too much, perhaps something had happened. Perhaps he had *done* something. Like I frequently did.

"It's not Matt." Damian shook his head. He stared at the floor for several long moments, then he seemed to force his head up to meet my gaze. "It's Ray. When Andrew— when he left you in there, he—" He choked up.

My heart and gut clenched painfully.

Mum glanced between us. "He was reversing his car, trying to get away in a hurry so he was going at full speed, and the back of his car crashed right into the driver's side of Ray's car."

Now I glanced between them. "Is he okay?" He couldn't be, not judging by the look on Damian's face.

"Where is he? What happened to him? You s-said An-Andrew was back in prison, so he must be o-okay." I was so afraid, so upset, I stuttered. Bloody hell.

"Ray wasn't, Joshua. He wasn't okay at all. It was quite an impact, right into the driver's side. Both cars are wrecks, but Andrew was sitting in front in his, so he walked away with minimal damage. Ray... he didn't walk away at all."

No! "No." It couldn't be. "Damian?"

He shook his head, staring down at our hands now.

"He's *dead*? Andrew *killed* him?"

"He did. I'm sorry, Joshua." Mum reached out to squeeze my arm, since my hand was still holding tight to Damian's.

That was the crash I'd heard right before I'd passed out. I'd hoped he'd wrapped his car around a lamp post, but it had been Ray's car... He'd been on his way home and Andrew had just rammed into him in his own selfish attempt to try and flee the scene after attempting to kill me. Which he hadn't succeeded in, but he'd killed Ray instead.

I wished he'd killed me, like he planned. Maybe if he had, he wouldn't have been driving away exactly when he did, maybe then Ray could still be alive. Matilda and Matt didn't have their dad anymore...

Damian didn't have his uncle, who had *been* like a father to him.

I cried for real now. It wasn't a shock. I seemed to spend half my time crying. Life was overwhelming, and my feelings to everything that happened to me in life was overwhelming.

Now more than ever.

I couldn't breathe, the sobs wrecked me.

Ray was dead. One bad experience, one meeting with Andrew, and he was *dead*. And here I was, living through his abuse for ten years, living through the wreck he left me, suicide attempts, and now his attempt to kill me—and I was *still* alive. It wasn't fair. It should be me, not him. Ray didn't deserve to suffer because of Andrew. He was my burden, my abuser, my nightmare, my biggest fear.

I couldn't calm down, still couldn't breathe. Panic was setting in. *Maybe I'm going to die anyway.*

"Josh. Josh, come on."

Someone was holding me. My face was pressed against a flat, hard chest. *Damian.* He was still here with me, and he wasn't leaving. He was the only one I had to live for—Mum too, of course, but she had someone else, a life without me. Damian had only me now, he needed me, and I couldn't turn into the mess I usually was.

Damian's world had turned tits up. This wasn't about me any more, it was all about him now.

I had to calm myself. For him. I couldn't fall apart when he was clearly on the edge. He'd always been here for me, supporting me, being patient with me.

It was my turn now. It had to be. I had to pay him back for everything I'd made him go through. All the shit, all the tantrums, all the paranoia, all the intense emotions always plaguing me.

I *had* to be strong. He needed me. For once in my life I needed to pull myself together, to be there for someone else. The past few years had been all about me—my entire life had been all about me, what with Andrew abusing me for as long as I could remember…

"Shh." Damian rocked us gently. "Breathe, come on, deep breaths."

It was a stuttering breath, but a breath none-theless. Another one, just as shaky. A third, a fourth — I lost count, but I eventually calmed down enough to wrap my arms around him and just holding on, hoping to give him my silent support and love.

Because I did love him. So much. I'd never loved anyone before, not before I met him. Thanks to me, we were always on a bit of a rocky ground, what with the smallest thing able to set me off… but I didn't ever want to be without him. He was my rock, my everything, the only thing in my life that made me get out of bed in the morning.

I *had* to pull myself together and be strong for him.

I could do that, couldn't I?

He stroked my back in big, soothing circles. It made me feel bad, because he was comforting me when I was the one who should be comforting him.

"I'm so sorry. This is all my fault. I never should've stayed there, not when I knew he was after me."

He drew in a sharp breath. I heard it, but also felt his chest rising. "I'm sorry for not believing you."

"We're sorry," Mum said quietly.

I couldn't expect anything else. I knew what my disorder comprised, I'd read all about it, everywhere I could find information about it. Paranoia was a common symptom. So were my intense emotions. Being borderline… I hated it. But I had to live with it. Some people might get better, might not fit the criteria any more, but as for me… I didn't think I'd ever get there. I was too messed up. And if it did happen, it would be years and years down the road.

"I never should've said yes to staying with them. If I hadn't, Ray'd be alive now."

Damian's soothing circles stopped for a second, before they started up again.

"You can't think like that, Joshua."

"How can I not? It's true."

"I know it's hard to hear—for both of you—but what happened, happened. Thinking what-ifs won't change anything. Nothing at all."

How could Mum be so calm and collected? A person who'd been a major part of my life was dead! Killed by her ex-husband, who had been trying his best to *kill* me. Being a solicitor had its advantages, perhaps.

I pulled back from Damian so I could look him in the eye. He seemed knackered and the whites of his eyes were bloodshot. "I'm so sorry." I teared up again, but fought to keep it back.

He seemed to have the same problem. "He was gone and you were—" He closed his eyes briefly. "You were hanging in there. They said we should prepare for the worst, Josh. The *worst*." Now there were tears, leaking slowly and trickling down his cheeks. "They didn't think you'd make it. They expected brain death, or at the very least brain damage."

"I'm already brain damaged." It slipped out. It was not the time to say that, though it was true. They said borderline personality disorder was a brain damage—it was like I had third-degree burns on my mind, because I had no skin to protect myself against the onslaught of emotion.

He swallowed again, whether because he was fighting tears or because he didn't like what I said, I couldn't tell.

He grabbed my arms, pulled me back in, and buried his face in the crook of my neck. Now it was my turn to rub soothing circles over his back. It felt weird, doing it, because I'd never done it before. I'd never had to comfort him before. It had always been him comforting me. Always me needing comfort because I couldn't handle being me and feeling what I was feeling.

Mum got up. I heard her heels clack on the floor, but when I turned my head to see what she was up to, she was already out the door. She'd left us alone.

"What about Matt?" What Silver said came back to me. "He found me... How's he holding up?"

"He's not saying anything." Damian's voice was muffled, teary. "Claire and Matilda are inconsolable, but Matt... nothing. I think maybe he's in shock."

Who wouldn't be? If he'd come home and found me, he must've first seen the cars. The cars that were wrecked and where his dad had died.

"Did he die instantly? Ray... He didn't suffer, did he?" I hoped he hadn't. That would make it even worse, because he was a kind, gentle person and he didn't—hadn't—deserved what happened to him.

Damian drew another stuttered breath. "No. Andrew's car hit the driver's side, yes. Ray was unconscious on impact, as far as I know. He died here in the hospital. Too much trauma, his body couldn't handle it."

"Matt— did he find Ray too?" God. Fifteen years old and experiencing this tragedy…

"No. The ambulance had already gone by the time Matt came home. Only the police and the fire engines were left. Ray and Andrew had both been driven to hospital. Andrew wasn't hurt so much, so he was escorted right back to prison. But Matt saw the cars, and I reckon he knew exactly what waited him. The copper I talked to said Matt hurried into the house. He came out holding the dog and yelling for them to come get you."

If any of us would need therapy after this, it was Matt. Right now I reckoned he needed it more than even I did. And I'd been going weekly to see my therapist for five years.

"It's not fair." I rested my cheek against the side of his head. "It's so not fair."

"No," he agreed quietly. "It's not fair."

TWO YEARS AGO

"*I* don't know what to wear."

"Wear whatever. It's just a dinner."

My blood instantly boiled. "I can't just wear whatever," I snapped. "This is a dinner with your family."

Unfair. That's what it was. Annoying. Irritating.

Why didn't I have anything nice in my closet?

I had nothing I felt would fit. I wanted to look my best for them, to show I wasn't so much of a mess. I was, obviously, but I didn't want them to wish Damian had never met me. That he'd met someone normal, someone who wasn't borderline.

"Josh, they're not going to care what you wear. Just pick whatever."

"No." I couldn't pick whatever. "What do you

223

think they're going to think about me if I show up in holey jeans and a plain jumper? Or joggers?" I shuddered at the thought. "They want you to be with someone worthy of you. I can't ever be that, so I have to at least look nice."

"They want me to be happy." He finally turned to me, buttoning his shirt. The look he gave me was one of patience. It made me angrier.

"Are you, though?" I hadn't meant to challenge him—but my emotions were boiling and it slipped out.

He just stared at me.

I sank onto the bed, despair washing in and distinguishing the boiling anger. "I don't know what to wear." I flopped back, stared at the ceiling. "I don't want to look like the mess I am."

He sat down next to me, put a hand tentatively on my knee. "It's not the end of the world."

"It is. It feels like it." It was my entire world right now, what to wear to the dinner. With Damian's family, the only family he had left, the family I wanted to like me, I wanted them to be happy for Damian, for us.

But here I was, unable to even find a proper outfit.

I wasn't ticking off much in the sanity department.

"Take your time, Josh. Calm down. We'll find something for you to wear later. We're not in a hurry." He squeezed my knee.

"Yeah. Okay." Easier said than done, though.

My emotions switched every which way all the time, but they could also linger. I felt this was one of those that wouldn't go away in a minute.

I rolled onto my side and curled up, with my back to Damian. He continued sitting there though, even though he wasn't touching me anymore.

Now that was calming. Him, so bloody patient with me, no matter what havoc I wreaked on myself or anyone else. He was just… there.

I knew he was. And nothing was better than that feeling, of knowing he would be here, no matter what. For now, anyway.

I couldn't foresee the future, but for now we were good. Maybe he would lose patience with me—who could blame him?—but for now he was the steady rock in my life. Him and Mum. They were collected, calm, down-to-earth. So alike from me, but then I didn't want anyone else to be like me, to feel everything as intense as I did. It was exhausting. Being me was exhausting.

But he was here. That helped tremendously.

CHAPTER 19

"Why hasn't Cooper been to see you?"

Damian levelled an unimpressed stare at me.

I shrugged. Looked down. Bit my lip.

"Everyone else's been here. Your family came up from Bristol to be here for you. They dropped everything and came up here the minute they found out what had happened." Damian turned away from me now. "They're here, your mum and her girlfriend are here, Chloe's here... but Cooper. He's strangely absent."

"Does he even know what happened?" Had anyone spoken to him? I certainly hadn't. I had spoken to everyone else, even Chloe—Claire's sister, who had grown up with them too, just like Damian.

Even Claire had been to see me, even if it had been a brief visit.

She and Damian weren't that close though, so it wasn't often I saw her, even though she lived in London too.

"I don't know. I haven't told him. I should think he'd spoken to his own bloody family." It was bothering him that Cooper hadn't been here. It didn't bother me so much. Cooper was Cooper: unreliable, selfish, all about living life to the fullest without a care for anyone else.

He had his reasons. I couldn't blame him. Not even for not visiting me, even though I could've died. Cooper wasn't a fan of hospitals—and considering what he was struggling with, who could blame him?

"Why do you just shrug it off? He's your family. He should be here with the rest of them." He turned his head away. I knew he was getting emotional again.

I couldn't blame him for that. Since I found out yesterday, I'd tried not to think about it, because I couldn't break down. I couldn't make this about me, because it wasn't.

"You can't come here and tell me you're fine with it. Everything that smacks of abandonment, whatever small or imaginary part, is a major trigger, so don't even try it with me."

He was right. I tried not to dwell on it though. "I know Cooper. I don't expect anything from him… I doubt he even knows. He's likely on a bender somewhere."

"He's not just your family, Josh, he's your mate."

"Yeah." Everyone was so hard on Cooper. They didn't even know… and yet they judged. I didn't— but then I knew. "It's just the way it is."

"It's selfish."

"I guess…" I didn't want to talk about Cooper.

A knock at the door saved me from it.

"Hey." Chloe stuck her head inside, and when she saw it was just me and Damian, she stepped inside fully. "How are you feeling?" It was directed at me.

"Okay." I was, actually. Beaten, yes, had a headache, yes. But I'd survived Andrew yet again, and it *did* feel good. He hadn't managed to break me this time either. Well, he had already broken me, but he hadn't managed to *shatter* me. I still wished it would've been me instead of Ray though… Life was unfair, so bloody unfair.

"Good. That's good." Chloe's mascara was smudged, her eyes a bit bloodshot. She'd obviously been crying.

Seeing it made it so much harder for me to hold back. *Again, Josh, this is not about you.* Easier said than done—because I loved them too.

"We have to go." Chloe jerked her head towards the doorway. "Final preparations and all. Claire's a mess. I reckon we have to do all the talking and organising."

"Yeah." Damian nodded once. He fumbled for my hand and squeezed tight once he found it. "I'll see you later, okay?"

"O-okay."

Chloe did a small movement that I supposed was a wave, then left with Damian. Damian pulled the door closed, but not all the way shut, so I watched their backs turn down the corridor.

I slid down in bed, unable to hold the tears back. They *ran* down my cheeks. The grief was so over-whelming I couldn't even sob, couldn't make a sound. Just the tears, wetting my cheeks, my chin, my pillow.

I'd never lost anyone before, not someone as close to me as Ray was to them. He was family to me now too, though not by blood as he'd been for Damian. Family by choice. I loved him. He'd been a part of my life almost as long as Damian had.

When a friend of mine had killed himself, jumped out in front of a car right in front of me, it had landed me in hospital. I hadn't been able to deal with it. A month in hospital, it had been. Over a month. It'd happened in November and I hadn't been out before the beginning of January.

I liked to think I was doing better than I had been back then. I was, wasn't I? I wasn't screaming my head off, I wasn't being dragged to hospital… I was *in* a hospital, but that was all Andrew's fault. It all came back to Andrew, every bloody time.

He hadn't just ruined my life now, but a whole lot of other peoples' lives too. Claire, Damian, Matilda, Matt, Chloe… Ray was their family by *blood*, he'd been a loving parent and guardian. He'd accepted *me*.

Now I would never see him again. Never speak to him, never go over to dinner and find him there at the table or helping Claire in the kitchen.

I curled up on my side, hands over my face to try and stem the tears. I wanted them to stop, I really did, but at the same time it felt good to get it all out. I was so tired of crying, of being a mess, of never being able to pull myself together or figure myself out.

It'd been five years since Andrew had been removed from my life. Since the police had escorted him out of my hospital room. Three years since he was finally put away. Three years since the last time I'd had to go into every detail of my life, of what it had been like for as long as I could remember.

I'd thought he was out of my life. Yet he managed

to come back into it—and he did *this*. Why couldn't he have been the one who died? No one deserved it better than him. He was a monster. A selfish, sadistic, perverted monster who got off on raping and hurting *kids*.

It was a wonder no one in prison had taken him out yet. It always happened on telly. A prisoner pulling a knife on another. Inmates killing inmates. Why couldn't it have happened to him? I wanted *him* to die, not for Ray to be dead. It just wasn't fair. Ray'd never done anything to deserve this, to deserve having *Andrew* rob him of his life. Rob two teenagers of their loving dad.

I hadn't seen Matilda or Matt yet. Damian was with me as much as he could, what with being there for Claire and helping plan a funeral and dealing with whatever all of it entailed. Chloe was staying with Claire, Matilda and Matt at the house. It must be horrible for them, worse than for anyone else.

Ray had been the love of Claire's life. Matilda and Matt were still teenagers, still in school, and now they didn't have a dad.

"Joshua?"

Mum put her hand on my shaking shoulder.

I didn't turn to face her. I couldn't, not like this. So I just pressed my hands to my face, hoping to hide the tears and the blotchiness I knew they caused. I was too familiar with crying not to know what I looked like while I did it.

"I can't do this."

Her fingers squeezed me. "You can't do what?"

"I can't be strong."

"No one's saying you have to be." The bed dipped slightly, telling me she'd sat down on the edge of it. She kept her hand on my shoulder.

"This is Damian's family. He should be allowed to lean on me for a change. But I just— I *can't!*"

"I don't think he expects that of you, Joshua. Ignoring your emotions to be there for him... we all know that's not you."

It wasn't at all. "You all know I'm an emotional wreck."

"We all know you feel emotions more intensely than we do. We can't even imagine what it must be like for you, especially at this time, when we feel the grief so intensely ourselves. For you it must be three times as bad."

My whole body hurt from the crying. The pillow was so wet it was soggy. "I want to be normal. I want to be able to have control of myself, to have some self-defense against this. I hate feeling out of control."

"I know." Mum sighed. "I know."

"I'm never going to get better." It hit me in the

gut, so much so I curled up further, my knees almost pressed against my chest and stomach now.

"You can't know that. People do get better, even with borderline personality disorder."

"Emotionally unstable personality disorder," I shot in. "Fits better. Tells people exactly what it is they're dealing with without them having to look it up."

She sighed again, squeezed my shoulder again. "People do get better from it, Joshua. They go to therapy, they learn techniques to deal with it, learn to turn their thoughts around so they can calm themselves. People *get* better. Some so much that they don't qualify as having borderline personality disorder anymore. It is possible. But it does take time."

"I've been in therapy for five years." How much longer could it take?

"Five years, ten years, fifteen… It's a long road."

The sobs hit me, right where it already hurt, in my gut, squeezing my chest tight. "I c-can't wait th-that long!"

"I'm afraid you don't have any other choice." Her hand travelled down to my upper arm, rubbing it. "And you know what? You *are* strong. You survive every day, every unstable emotion. You *survive*, Joshua, and that's more than can be said for many others with your disorder. You're strong—and we all appreciate that, we all know how you struggle. Not because we can empathise with it, because we have no idea what it's like being you, but we *see* it. We see the struggle, we see how much you want to be there for and with Damian. We see that you *do* want to live."

"I just tried to k-kill myself. Well, An-Andrew just tried to kill me, but b-before that—"

"That's the impulsivity. The most dangerous of your symptoms. But you survived that too, just like you did five years ago. You survive, Joshua, and for that you are *so* strong."

I mulled over that. It didn't sound like me, being strong, but the rest of it… Maybe she had a point. I always survived. I struggled every day—mostly every day—and I was still here, alive and breathing and healthy.

"Do you think he's going to leave me?"

"Damian?"

"Yeah."

Another sigh, this one different from the ones earlier. This one was full of impatience with me. "No, I don't think he will."

"But they need him now."

"They can have him without him having to leave you, you know. Just because someone else might depend on him now, doesn't mean you can't still do it too." She didn't stop rubbing my arm. "I know these abandonment issues are also part of your disorder, but you need to get it inside your head that he's not going to leave. I'm not going to leave. No one's going to leave you. You'll always have us, even when you hate us."

My body shook as I drew in a deep breath. "I don't hate anyone. Except for An-Andrew. He deserves it."

"I know he does. And I know you don't hate any of us, but that black-and-white thinking... Staying positive as long as someone treats you nicely, gives you all their attention, but quickly switching to negative at perceived criticism or hurtfulness. The quick shift from idealising to devaluing, it can make it seem like it sometimes. And I know that for you, that doesn't happen often, but it *has* happened. It's part of the disorder, it's not something you can control, but it can be stressful and hurtful to us too. We don't mean to make that switch happen, but sometimes not even we, who're closest to you, can't help it."

Without even thinking my actions through, I turned over and wrapped my arms around her, hugging her tight. She stiffened, then awkwardly patted my back. She wasn't good with affection, Mum, but she tried for me. For the first fifteen years of my life I hadn't had much of a relationship with her at all. It did feel good to finally have it now though. She was a good Mum. She'd just trusted the wrong person to take care of me while she'd been busy with her career, busy making a life for us where we didn't have to worry about money. Not that we'd been lacking *ever*, considering grandma came from a well-off family, but still.

"I love you, Mum." I told Damian all the time, but it wasn't often I told her. I needed to tell her, and I hoped it was something she needed to hear. Or appreciated to hear.

"I love you too." It came out a bit strained.

I couldn't blame her. Mum had never been an affectionate person. She was cool, calm, always practical. She was not, however, someone who frequently spoke about her feelings. Maybe she did with Harriet, but hardly ever with me. The first time I'd actually seen her cry was back after my first suicide attempt, after Andrew had been arrested, when she'd told me about her own abuse. Abused by her own father. That was worse than being abused by my step-father. I couldn't even imagine. Your own flesh and blood.

Andrew was once again in prison. But at the cost of Damian's uncle, the only relative he had left who was older than him. Ray was dead, because of Andrew, because of Andrew's obsession with me.

"I wish it'd been me." It came out a whisper.

Mum tensed up, so she must've heard me. I didn't know if I'd meant for her to or not. She wrapped her arms around me, wrapped them tight— and she just held me.

*T*here was blood everywhere.

The tub, the toilet, the sink, the floor—all dotted red.

I lay on my back on the floor, the fluffy rug a nice place to rest on. I stared at the ceiling, but didn't actually see it. The pain in my arms held me grounded, held me firmly in place inside myself.

As long as I felt the pain, I couldn't flit away. I couldn't leave, I couldn't give up, I couldn't die. I was still alive—as long as I felt the pain. I wanted to be alive, I really did, but it was hard. Living was so bloody hard.

A startled gasp could be heard, but it hardly registered. It didn't matter. All that mattered was the pain.

I focused on that. What else could I do? It kept me alive.

"Josh?"

Why was someone calling me? Didn't they realise I was fighting a battle here? A battle I couldn't lose. I had to win it. They had to let me fight it.

Someone slapped my face.

"Josh?"

"I'm ringing for an ambulance. He's lost a lot of blood, mate."

I didn't know what the answer was to that. Did Damian think Silver was right? Had I lost that much blood?

My face was slapped again.

"Don't—"

"Josh, come on."

I couldn't come on. It didn't work like that. He didn't know what it was like to relive my life in my dreams every night. To wake up in a cold sweat, terrified that my life up till now had been the dream and that when I did wake up, it would be Andrew next to me instead of Damian.

"They're on their way, D."

Another slap to the face.

"Stop!"

"Come on, Josh, stay with me."

I didn't want to stay anywhere. Well, okay, I

wanted to stay with him, of course I did, but everything hurt. Not just the outside, but the inside. So
much I couldn't breathe.

I wanted that to stop. That on the inside.

But it didn't. It never did.

I was stuck with it.

Forever.

CHAPTER 20

J was wound so tight I felt I was seconds away from breaking.

It felt unreal to see Damian locking us into Ray and Claire's house. We'd never have to use a key before, it had always been open and welcoming.

"Aren't they home? Claire, and Matt, and Matilda?" My palms were sweaty. I tried wiping them on my joggers, but it didn't help.

"They are." Damian pulled the key back out and pushed the door open. "But we keep the doors locked now."

He didn't look at me, I didn't think he even gave a thought to it, but that simple reminder brought me back to that day—

I'd been alone, it'd just been me and the dog. And

then he'd been there. He'd got in through the veranda door, which should've been locked. It could've been one of them who had forgot to lock it —or it could've very well been me. All I knew was that *that* day was the worst day of my life. Well, in the last five years, anyway.

And it would also be the worst day in Claire, Matt and Matilda's lives. While Claire had popped in for a quick visit at the hospital, Matilda and Matt had not, so I didn't know what would greet me. I couldn't blame them for not coming to see me. Their dad had just died.

What would I be walking into now? Did they blame me? Did they think it was my fault Ray died? Or were they so devastated that there could be nothing else on their mind?

"Stop it."

I startled. "What?" Looking at Damian, I found him scrutinising me.

"Stop worrying. I can see you're doing it, and just — just stop." He sounded so resigned.

"I'm sorry." I bent to put my shoes away properly.

"Josh…" Damian grabbed me once I straightened up and crushed me in a hug. "You better not leave me."

"I won't." I linked my arms behind his back, a bit

confused as to this major show of affection, and major show of worry. "I *won't* leave you. You better not leave me either." There was always the possibility of him growing tired of me and my emotions and my bullshit, but I'd never get tired of him. He was my *rock*. If I didn't have him to hold on to, I'd drown. I'd shatter into a million pieces and there'd be no way to put me back together.

"You just can't leave me, Josh. Not in any sort of way."

I read him loud and clear. No more suicide attempts. No anything that could lead to me leaving him.

"No. I can't." I buried my face in his neck. "I don't want to, not ever."

"Good." Another tight squeeze, then he abruptly let me go.

I watched silently as he shrugged out of his jacket and put his shoes in place, then I followed him further into the house, dreading what I would meet, what I would see, what they would say.

Claire and Matilda was curled up on the biggest sofa, while Chloe was on the smaller one. All three of them stared at the telly that was on low volume. I didn't think they actually watched it, though, that they'd simply put it on for show. Matt was conspicuously missing.

"Where's Matt?"

I didn't think that was the best way to open the dialogue for Damian, but he did get their attention.

"In his room." Matilda sighed, curled up on herself, and wrapped her arms around her knees. "Been there for hours. Just him and Storm."

Should I say something? Hi, maybe? But Damian had already announced our arrival, already started up the conversation, and it felt silly to say hi now. Instead I stood by awkwardly, hardly daring to look at them. Socially awkward, that was me. Usually it was Damian, I was a lot more sociable than him. It was thanks to me we even had mates outside of Silver and Kian. Yet, now... this whole situation was partly my fault.

Damian took a step forward towards them, away from me. With him not blocking my sight anymore, I could see the kitchen out of the corner of my eye. *Don't look. Don't look!* But I did. And there it was. The table. Where he'd beat my head against. Where he'd left me to die. And between the kitchen and the sofas were the veranda door. That's where he'd come in—

No. No no no.

I took a step backwards.

He'd been in here. With me, while I'd been here alone. He'd hurt me, tried to kill me, had nearly succeeded, and he *had* killed Ray, and it was *not* okay—

I took another step backwards.

I knew, rationally, he was back in prison and couldn't come through the veranda door again… but my mind was rarely rational.

Another step back.

"Josh?"

Damian had turned around and he now watched me curiously.

"I can't—" My gaze flickered to the kitchen table. Maybe I imagined it, but a flash of pain shot through my skull.

His brows furrowed.

"I'm sorry." I shook my head. *I wanted to be strong.* But I wasn't. I never was. I could never *be* strong. "I just— I can't."

I ran out of there like my heels were on fire.

"Josh!"

He'd followed me.

When I turned from where I was crouched over in the driveway, he stood just outside the door.

"I'm so sorry." I was such a mess. Why did I always have to be such a mess?

He pressed his lips together, throat working as he swallowed. "Where are you going?"

Going? "I don't know." I didn't have a plan. All I

knew was I needed to get out of that house. "Home. Or to Mum's. I don't know. But I can't—"

"I get it," he cut me off. "But I've got to stay."

Of course he had to. That didn't mean it didn't hurt. I wanted him with me, but— the people in there were his family. They were hurting. He couldn't run after me and my messed-up mind. Not *now*.

"Yeah." *Of course you have to. I don't blame you. Much, anyway.*

I walked away.

CHAPTER 21

I knocked on the door, frantic. No one answered, but I didn't give up. *He has to be here. He has to!*

Eventually I saw lift turn on from the tinted window, and then the door pulled open. Cooper emerged, with tousled, blond hair, and face split in a wide yawn. His chest was bare, he was only clad in loose-hanging pyjama trousers.

Once he finished his yawn and opened his eyes to peer at me, I saw they were bloodshot.

"Where've you been?"

He swayed a little. "I'm right here."

He's drunk. "Ray's dead."

"What?" He rubbed his eyes.

"Ray. Damian's uncle. He's dead." He had no

idea. His facial expression was blank. "Haven't you spoken to anyone recently?"

"No." He let go off to the door. It swung open, admitting me into his flat. "Why should I?"

"Because he's *dead*."

"He's not my family." He yawned again as he walked into the living room, where he dropped onto the sofa.

I stood in front of him, staring down at his drunken form. "*I* nearly died. Twice."

He blinked, a bit more alert. "What? When? How?"

"I swallowed all my pills." And failed at doing what I was supposed to do. *Always a failure*. "And then Andrew tried to kill me."

He sat up straight. "*What*?!"

"I told everyone he was after me, but no one believed me." I hung my head. "And then he came for me. At Ray and Claire's house..." I couldn't go on. It hurt too much. It left me too much of a frightened mess.

Cooper peered up at me. There was almost no white left in his eyes.

It worried me.

"Are you okay?"

"Me? Yeah. Awesome." He rubbed at his eyes again. Maybe they itched. Surely they must, what with the way they looked. "Fell asleep with my contact lenses in."

"Are they still in?" It didn't seem comfortable.

"Well, yeah. Else I wouldn't be able to see much, would I?"

True.

"Everyone's here, you know." I sank down on the sofa next to him. "Everyone's been to see me. They're all here for the funeral."

"When's that?" His nose scrunched up. Because his family was here, or because of the funeral, I had no idea.

"Tomorrow."

He fell back again. "Now you mention it, there's been a lot of activity on my phone lately."

"Why haven't you answered?"

"Don't want to talk to any of them." He sighed.

I sighed too. "I met him. Face to face."

"Who?" A beat of heavy silence, then— "Andrew?"

I nodded.

"Shit."

"Yeah." I couldn't stop seeing him in my mind, how he'd looked standing there. He hated me for what I'd done to him, but he had no right to. I was the one with the right to hate—and I *did*. I hated him so much I didn't even have words to convey it properly.

Then the waterworks started. *Again.*

Cooper patted me awkwardly on the shoulder, but otherwise stayed quiet.

I was grateful.

"I w-want to g-go b-back." It had plagued me ever since I left.

"Go back where?"

"To Ray and Claire's house." Why couldn't I have been strong enough to push past my own traumatic recollection? I wanted to be there for them, to be *with* them. With Damian. Yet I'd left. I'd gone all the way into the city to see Cooper, of all people. Damian would not be pleased.

"Then go back," he said, matter of fact.

He made it sound so simple. *It isn't.* "He got in. Through the veranda door." Just the thought of his voice made me shiver in fright. "He hit my head against their kitchen table. He left me on the floor to die." My breath came out shaky as the images, the memories, played through my mind.

Cooper's breath hitched, but that was the only indication he gave that my words moved him. "Go back, Josh."

No!

"You have to go back there. Face your fears. You've got to."

I couldn't believe what I was hearing. "This coming from *you*?"

"We're different. *Quite* different." He turned his head, bloodshot eyes meeting mine. "For once, I don't have a brain injury. Or a mental illness. Whatever the fuck it is."

I wanted to snap back. I knew *his* secret, I knew what was wrong with *him*. But the words wouldn't come. I turned away instead.

"Josh…" He sighed. "I'm sorry. But I do think you should go back. Be with the people who matter."

"I think you should talk to your family."

He snorted in contempt. "I don't think so. I'm better off on my own. But you… you're not. So go *back*. You can't stay here."

Knife to the heart. "Why not?" I could always stay with Cooper. He never minded.

"Because I don't want to wake up from this hangover tomorrow and find you dead in my bathroom." He delivered it softly, but matter-of-factly. "Andrew almost killed you. He managed to kill Damian's uncle. I *can't* be responsible for you. I'm not even good at being responsible for myself."

This must be the alcohol talking. Cooper would not be so emotional without it. But he had a point. He was the most irresponsible person I knew—and what with my borderline and what that entailed… This was not a good time to stay with him.

"You have to leave." He dropped his head back to rest against the sofa. "You've got to, Josh. Go to your mum, if you don't want to go back there. But go somewhere that's not *here*."

I know when I'm not wanted. I know he's right.

"Yeah."

"Good."

Silence descended over us as I clutched at my knees. I didn't want to leave, to go out there amongst all the people, to head through the city again… but I had to.

I didn't know where I'd go. Mum's place wasn't that far off, but Damian… I wanted Damian.

But did I want him enough to go back to that house?

I KNOCKED SOFTLY.

The house was dark by now. It was late, but not *that* late. Then again, we all had to be up early in the morning to face the hardest day of their lives. Well, one of the hardest days. Could the funeral trump the day Ray had died? Probably not. But it would probably be close.

There was a snick as the door unlocked and opened, and then Claire's pale face peeked through the slit.

"Hey." I buried my hands in the pockets of my hooded jumper awkwardly.

"Josh." She let the door slide open further. "They've all gone to bed."

I only nodded as I shuffled over the threshold. I didn't know what to say to her. Sorry maybe, but it didn't feel right. It didn't feel *enough*.

"You should go downstairs. Be with him." She closed and locked the door as soon as I was inside, then wrapped her arms around herself. Her eyes were just as bloodshot as Cooper's had been, but she'd been crying. He'd just been drunk and worn his contacts too long. She had a legitimate reason for looking like hell. She'd just lost her *husband*.

A fist squeezed around my heart, paralysing me in fear for a moment. *It could've been Damian. What if it had been Damian?* I would've been locked up in the madhouse and never been let out again. Without him, what did I have?

"Goodnight," I murmured, then hurried downstairs to check he was really there and alive.

I needn't have been so afraid. He was asleep, yes, but his chest rose and fell noticeably under the duvet.

I let out a relieved sigh. *What did you think?* A voice in my head said. *That he'd died the few hours you've been away?*

You can never be sure of anything. Least of all that the people you love will always be there. I walked over to the bed slowly. Sat down as gently as I could, then leaned back until I lay down too.

He didn't stir. *Good. He must be exhausted.*

I tried to sleep, I really did. But sleep didn't come. Not even close. My mind was too busy to settle down. Too busy with *everything*; Damian, Claire, Matilda, Matt, Andrew, being in a coma, how that must've been for everyone, Ray dead, funeral tomorrow, who knew what the days after would hold, what would happen then—

I got out of bed. I felt all jittery and if I stayed I'd be tossing and turning, and would eventually wake Damian. He needed to sleep. He'd had a hell of a week—*over* a week. I'd been in a coma, Ray dead, and he'd had to take care of Claire, Matilda, and Matt and plan a funeral. Chloe too, of course, but she was more emotional than Damian. He kept it inside.

I couldn't stay in the room. I'd pace, and that would wake him too, so I headed upstairs. All was dark, the house was silent. Everyone else was asleep.

I was all alone on the ground floor, just me and my messed up mind, alone in the darkness.

That never boded well.

The kitchen called to me. It didn't have a door, just an arch, and I stared in through it, straight at the drawers. The drawers containing cutlery. More specifically, knives. I resolutely refused to look towards the kitchen table.

I wasn't even aware I moved. One moment I was standing next to the door leading back to the basement, next I was pulling the top-most drawer open.

There were a lot of knives. Black handles, silver blades. They glinted in the weak lightning. They really did call to me, begged to be used.

Cutting... I hadn't done it in a while now. Not that the previous cuts had healed completely. Though the stitches had been taken out—while I was in a *coma*, but I pushed that thought away—my arms were still red and sore and the stitches themselves had left more scars on my skin. They joined the rest, the crisscrossing of all of them. Self-inflicted scars, scars from stitches being out there to hold my mutilated skin together...

I didn't want more. But I *did*. Cutting was... it was a part of me. I couldn't stop. It was like a drug. I was addicted—addicted to the feel and the pain and the blood and the scars. They'd never go away—and

I hated them, often, but sometimes I liked them. I hated them when they reminded me of everything that had happened to me, everything Andrew had done. But I liked them when they reminded me of how they'd kept me alive.

They'd been the only thing keeping me alive.

Andrew had nearly killed me.

Four days in a coma.

That was *serious*. He'd never done that to me before, so that was certainly a first. *I guess there's a first time for anything.* Oh so cliché, but oh so true.

My fingers slid around a black handle. The silver blade held me transfixed. I pulled up my sleeve. Pressed the blade against the scars. *I shouldn't do this. I shouldn't. I have to be my best tomorrow. If not for me, then for Damian. I can't be a mess, I* can't. But I was a mess, and the only way I knew to calm myself was this.

I cut.

CHAPTER 22

"*J*osh?"

The knife cluttered to the ground, dripping blood onto Claire's clean floors. I flattened myself against the wall, my mind going *caught! caught! caught!*.

"Josh?"

The panic subsided, just so, and I realised I wasn't actually in any kind of danger. In danger of utter humiliation, yes, but nothing else.

"Matilda?" I stared up at her.

She stared back down at me. She was only in a pair of really short shorts, with a shirt that must be triple her size on over it. Her arms were wrapped around her waist, her hair hung loosely down her back and over her shoulders. Her face was void of any traces of make-up. There were, however, traces of tears.

Her gaze moved from me to the knife. After a few seconds, her focus was solely on my arms. My bared arms. Bared, scarred, and bleeding.

"Is this where it happened?"

What? "What?" What'd happened here? Bleeding, sure. Lots of it.

"Your step-dad—I mean, well…" She moved her weight from one foot to the other. "Was it the kitchen that he—well… got you? They don't really speak in front of me, but I heard them mention there were blood in here."

Andrew. In this house. Grabbing me, in front of the veranda door. And then… then he'd hit my head against the kitchen table. The kitchen table that was right there. I stared at it, at the edge of it where my head must've made quite an impact. Was there blood on it still? I'd been bleeding, hadn't I?

Who'd had to clean that up?

My chest constricted painfully.

"I'm sorry." Matilda crouched down next to me. I hadn't even noticed her moving. "I shouldn't have brought that up. I'm sorry."

It was ridiculous to feel panicked and terrified. Andrew had hounded me for ten years, gone away, and he'd come back for an encore… but now he was gone again. They'd keep him gone now. He wouldn't hurt me again. *They said so last time too, yet he still had.* But not now. Now he wouldn't. Now he'd rot in jail. He'd murdered someone. One person. He'd tried for two. Or tried for one, really, and ended up with someone else. Certainly that couldn't be ruled an accident?

"I'm so sorry." A lump formed in my throat, making my voice choked. "I never should've come here to stay with you."

"I'm blaming him, Josh, not you. That sick fucker —" I could tell she wanted to continue cursing him , but she couldn't actually come up with anything else. She was raised properly, she was. Cursing wasn't something I'd ever heard her do.

Silence fell. I stared at the table. Matilda stared at the floor.

"I don't know all that's happened to you, but from what I've gathered before, it wasn't good. From what I've seen now, from the wreckage he left here, I know it must've been horrible." She draped the shirt over her knees that she drew tight to her chest. "How do you deal with it? With everything he did to you, and for so long... how do you manage to live a normal life? How do you *deal*? Because I don't know how to go on from this." She sounded so heartbroken, so lost, so desperate.

"This is how I deal." I nudged the knife with my foot. "It's not recommended. But it kept me alive. I'll leave it up for discussion whether that's a good thing or not."

She blinked, taking my words in, then her expression hardened. "Of course it's a good thing if the alternative is you ending up dead! No one deserves to die, especially not at the hands of someone else. And yes, you do it to yourself, but if you hadn't you say you'd be dead... that means he would've killed you, if you hadn't had that outlet." She motioned to the knife. "And that's just— it's not *right*. It is a good thing that you're here."

"If I hadn't been here your dad—"

"Dad loved you." She cut me off effectively. "You were family to him. You are to us. You're with Damian. Mum and Dad never thought he'd ever find anyone, and then he shows up with you... You're a mess, but he's *happy*."

Now the lump was back because her words moved me. "They told you this?"

"No. But they don't always realise I'm close enough to hear. Sometimes they like to talk over my head, like I'm still a little girl who can't understand what the grown-ups are talking about." She rested her head back against the wall. "*Didn't. Liked*. I hate it, having to talk about Dad in past tense. It's so… so bloody *final*."

It was. "Yeah."

"Cutting's the only thing that got you through?"

It seemed she wasn't done with the topic. "No. I wrote journals. Lots of them. All the time."

"Did you stop writing them?"

"Yeah…" I'd never meant to stop, but there had been big lapses in time, and eventually I'd just never got back to it. "I miss it. But it doesn't help. What's the point of writing things in a book that only I'm going to see? I already know how I feel. I don't need more reminders of it."

She bent forward and picked up the knife. She turned it around in her hand, studied the bloodied blade. I wanted to take it from her, to throw it away, to tell her to never look at it. But I didn't. Instead I just sat there, watching her out of the corner of my eye.

"Why don't you start a blog?"

"A blog?"

"Yeah, a blog. You know, like a journal, only digital and in the public domain. Some people find it more therapeutic to share on a blog where other people can comment and share their stories as well."

It wasn't the worst idea, I'd give her that. "Do you have a blog?"

"Yeah."

"What do you have to write about for therapeutic purposes?" As far as I knew, Matt was the only one showing signs of depression. Matilda had always been happy, well-liked, busy with her friends and after-school activities.

"Nothing. I write a blog simply because I like to share. Daily outfits, what shoes I bought, what food I ate, what book I read. That kind of stuff. Nothing deep. But I follow blogs where people share personal things from their life. Real deep and meaningful texts. This one girl is battling eating disorders. She finds it helps to write a blog, to hear from other people in the same situation, or just from people who wish her well." Matilda shrugged. "You're always on your laptop. What do you do on it?"

"Trying to write a book." It was going abysmal.

She turned to me, attention piqued. "What kind of book?"

"Fiction, mostly, but, you know… drawing from my own life. So maybe a bit auto-biographical too. I don't know. I haven't got that far in it."

Matilda put the knife back on the floor. "I guess I've got more serious things to blog about now."

She sure had. "Writing used to help. Along with therapy. Talking about it… I used to be in group therapy too."

She eyed me wryly. "Start a blog. Then you can process things in your own home instead of having to look everyone in the eye. I don't want to look anyone in the eye now. Everyone's going to be so sorry for me, or tell me it's going to get better, or what I *can* do to make it better. It doesn't feel like it's ever going to get better."

What could I say to that? It was six years since my life had got better, except not by much. Everything that had happened before still plagued me, by nightmares, flashbacks, or just all around anxiety. "It's not going to. Ever." I'd have to live with my past. It wasn't ever going to go away. Unless I got amnesia, but what were the odds? Or if I got Alzheimers in my old age. Or no… If I got that and reverted back to childhood, I would live it all over again.

"I don't know what we're going to do now." She looked so small, so fragile. "In less than twelve hours it'll all be so *final*. I don't think it's quite sunk in yet, you know, but once Dad's in the ground… it will. And what're we supposed to do then? I don't think Mum's going to be able to keep it together afterwards. She's barely keeping it together now. Matt and I are both in school. I don't even know how Matt's holding up, since he's cooped up in his room. We can't take care of ourselves."

I bit my lip. What could I say to that? I was

twenty-one years old, mostly unable to take care of myself, on disability because my diagnosis currently made it impossible for me to get a proper job. No education, no *nothing*. I couldn't help her—them. I couldn't even help myself.

"Damian and Chloe—even Mum—say we shouldn't worry. I don't see how we *can't* though. I mean, Mum's got a good job and all, but this house…" She looked around. "It's a big house. Probably expensive. I know they haven't paid it off. I've heard them talk about money." She swallowed. "I don't think Mum's going to be able to afford to keep the house on her own. So where are we going to live? Where are we going to *go*? I mean, they've probably got life insurance—not that Mum talks to me about it —but… I don't know. Maybe we could sue? He broke the rules, didn't he? He *killed* Dad."

Well, she was certainly more in-tune with all this than I was. I didn't even know what to say, because what she'd just rattled off, I hadn't even thought about. Yes, I reckon a house was expensive, and the debt they must have on it… I had no idea what would happen now. At all.

I was woefully ignorant. I'd never had to worry about this. Mum had always earned well, and even if she hadn't, Grandma came from money so it wasn't like our family would ever be poor.

"Have you ever experienced anyone dying before? Someone close to you?"

"No." No one in my family. "Yes." My thoughts went back three years, to Mal and the friendship I'd thought we'd started to build. Only he'd thrown himself in front of a car. After shoving me out of the way so I couldn't stop him. That had landed me in hospital for over a *month*. Mal had been even more of a mess than me. Maybe it was better for him now, not to live with all the horrible things he'd experienced. As far as I knew, he hadn't actually had anyone of his own. Not like I, who'd had Mum and then Damian.

"How'd they die?"

Should I tell her? It might not be good, all things considered, but I couldn't lie either. "He jumped in front of an oncoming car." Ray hadn't jumped though, he'd been the victim of a car-crash through no fault of his own.

"Oh."

Heavy silence.

"He was like me. Borderline. Emotionally unstable. Except his past was even worse than mine. I didn't think that was possible, but in group therapy… well, you hear a lot of stories. A lot of shit. A lot of messed-up things."

Matilda closed her eyes. I caught sight of tears squeezing their way underneath her lids to trickle down her cheek. "I get suicide. Some say it's selfish to do that, but I don't know— If you really, *really* don't want to live, then suicide is better, isn't it? But Dad... he wanted to live. He had lots of things to live for. That he was taken from us in that way— *that* I don't get. It's not fair."

"No. It isn't." Seeing her crying made it all the more difficult to hold back my own tears. Holding back was not one of my strengths. Usually it all came tumbling out in a waterfall of tears and tantrums and neediness and desperation and impulsivity.

She cried silently, the only sign of it was the tears and her trembling. I didn't know what to do, if there was anything I could do to make her feel better, so I simply sat there with my hands in my lap. The blood still trickled, my joggers absorbing it as it fell.

This was us: bonding on the kitchen floor. Bleeding, crying, grieving.

And tomorrow... tomorrow was going to be even worse.

I WOKE TO AN EMPTY BED. The other side was cold, so Damian must've already been up a while. I sat up and rubbed my eyes, wondering what time it was. I'd been up so late. I hoped I hadn't overslept.

No… Damian would've woken me if that was the case.

Then again, light was filtering through the window, bathing the room in bright light.

I threw my feet off the edge of the bed. My joggers were discarded on the floor and I sighed as I saw the blood stains. Damian must've seen them too, they stood out bright against the grey.

My bag lay at the foot of the bed, and I bent over to fish a new pair out of it. When I saw my suit, I sighed, because I'd forgotten to hang it up. Now it was probably wrinkled.

Once I'd hung it up on, I finally ventured upstairs. What awaited me now?

Silence, was what. Damian was at the table, elbows on the wood, and head in his hands. Breakfast stood untouched in front of him.

"Morning." I couldn't get myself to say *good morning* because it sure wasn't. This would be a very hard day.

Damian didn't answer.

I went to his side, bent to kiss his temple, and then positioned myself behind him to rub at his tense shoulders. *I can be a good boyfriend. I can do this. Be of support.* Pep-talks never helped me. Perhaps this would be the first.

"Anyone else up?"

"Chloe's in the living room. Matilda made breakfast and retreated to her room. Claire... I don't know."

"What about Matt?" I still hadn't seen or heard him. Nor had I seen or heard Storm. Was she still locked up in Matt's room too?

Damian only shook his head.

I retreated to the kitchen counter to make breakfast for both myself and for Matt. If he wouldn't come down, I'd bring it up. Damian had done that for me many times when I'd been too depressed to get out of bed.

A tentative knock on Matt's door turned up no answer. "Matt?" I knocked again, but when he still didn't answer, I tried the know. The door swung open.

Matt was lying stretched out on his bed, staring at the ceiling. Storm's little, fluffy body was curled up against his waist.

"I made you breakfast." I held the plate and glass of milk out, both to show him and hoping he'd take it.

He didn't.

I put it on his nightstand.

Matt didn't so much as move a muscle.

I looked down at him. Just about to start college, still underage, and having lost his dad. I knew I'd feel pretty helpless if I ever lost Mum, but I couldn't even begin to fathom how he must feel right now.

I felt completely out of my depth. Was this how Mum had felt back when she'd found out about the abuse? About what her husband was capable of? Back when I'd been so depressed and self-destructive and suicidal I hadn't known what was up and what was down? It was awful not knowing what to do. Not knowing what would be an appreciated gesture and what would not be.

"I'm here if you want to talk." Talking had helped me. Maybe it still could? Matilda's suggestion of a blog was fresh in my mind.

There was no answer from Matt. No acknowledgement.

"Please eat." I glanced at the food. Glanced back at him. I doubted he would, but at least I'd tried. That was all I could do.

I turned and left the room, Storm now following in my footsteps, yawning wide.

I felt rather helpless.

"*D*amian!"

I all but threw my laptop to the side as I stood. It landed on the sofa next to me, thankfully, but I was too happy to bother with it.

"What?" Damian came out from the kitchen, drying his hands on a dish towel. "You all right?"

I nodded enthusiastically. "I got in. I actually got in!" I couldn't believe it, but it was right there on the laptop. "I haven't got my A-levels results back yet, they're supposed to be out tomorrow, but they have to be good because I got an unconditional offer." I stared down at the screen for a moment, just to make sure it really was an unconditional offer before I looked back at Damian. "I got into university." I'd never thought that would happen. This time last year

I'd failed my A-levels. Now here I was, about to be a university student.

He smiled. "I told you, you could do it."

"Not without you." I hugged him. After doing so exceptionally bad at my A-levels last year, as had already been predicted, he'd helped me study. Even though he had a lot of studying to do on his own. "I couldn't have done it without you."

"I hardly did anything."

"You did." I drew back so I could look up at him. "You helped me, you motivated me, and it's thanks to you I managed this. That I managed to finish. Even after the hospitalisation from November to January... you got me through it. Everything I missed."

Without him I would've failed again, I knew it. If it hadn't been for him, I would've given up after my hospitalisation. Losing Mal, losing so much of college —over a month of non-attendance... He'd kept me motivated.

And now I could start university.

I'd never imagined I could ever get this far.

CHAPTER 23

There was a deep, rectangular hole in the ground. That's where the coffin would go.

Actually seeing it lowered, put into a dark hole, and knowing that it would soon be filled up by dirt again… it was not a good feeling.

Everyone would die in the end. Some would end up in a coffin, like Ray. Others would be cremated

Everyone would end up like this, one way or another. Everyone would die sometime. Even if they'd end up in the ground or cremated, everyone would die. It was a fact of life. I'd tried my best to die a few times, but I'd always failed at it. Now, staring down at the hole in the ground, I was glad I'd failed.

What if it had been me lying dead in a coffin,

being dropped into a hole and then covered with dirt? Maggots would start eating through, everything would rot eventually, until only bones were left...

I turned my back on the sight, horrified at my own thoughts. *This is about them. It's not about me.* Everything wasn't about me—today *nothing* was about me.

Damian was standing still at my side, staring at what was going on. All stone-faced. He and Mum could join a club with that, win a bloody championship.

Speaking of Mum, she was to the side of me. She stood behind Matilda and Matt. Chloe was at their other side with her boyfriend. When I'd first met her, she'd had a girlfriend. I'd thought she was gay, but such had not been the case after all. Maybe this was me, black-and-white thinking again. There was either straight or gay, no bi in-between. Ridiculous. My thinking pattern, that was. I *was* ridiculous.

Claire stood at Damian's other side with a handkerchief pressed to her face. Her thin shoulders shook.

Mum reached out to squeeze my arm. I tried for a smile but didn't manage it. When her hand fell away I slowly turned back around. I stepped closer to Damian, slipping my hand around his, squeezing.

He squeezed back, but his full focus was on the

grave in front of us. Matilda was crying at my side, big sunglasses unable to hide the torrent of tears. Matt… still no emotion. Chloe was also crying, leaning against Graeme.

Everyone grieved in their own way. There were friends of Ray and Claire here—they had a lot of them, though none I'd ever met. My family were here; all the way from Bristol to come see me in hospital. They'd all met Ray, they all knew how important he and Damian were to me. They were here for support.

Grandma stood at Mum's side. Harriet stood on the other, also there for support. Even though she was my mum's girlfriend, she was mostly there for Damian. He'd worked for her for so many years— they were as close as Damian could ever get to anyone who wasn't me or Silver. He and Kian were here too.

It crawled on. I didn't hear what anyone was saying, it was like I'd checked out completely. Except this wasn't what my dissociative episodes were like at all—because I still saw and took notice, it was just it all seemed to have been put on mute.

We were back at the house once it was over. Claire was now the one who was stone-faced. Chloe was crying on her boyfriend's shoulder. Matilda sat miserable at the kitchen table, hands wrapped around a mug filled with tea. Damian was sitting opposite her, also stone-faced. Matt had disappeared to his room. He hadn't brought the dog this time though, because she currently weaved around my legs. And me? I moved on auto-pilot. Or stumbled around on auto-pilot.

I couldn't do it anymore. I needed to be alone. I needed to calm down, I needed peace. Once I filled Storm's bowl with kibble, I headed down to the basement. No one stopped me. No one spoke to me. No one so much as looked at me.

The mattress bounded as I dropped down on it.

It was soft. Not quite familiar, but it felt good nonetheless. I lay across it, cheek against the duvet I'd been using, feet hanging off the edge. I stared at the wall. It was light, smooth, calming. No disruptions or glaring colours or patterns. All soothing.

I needed that. I needed something with nothing to focus on.

I needed to check out for a bit.

"*W*hat is the point?"

Damian sat down on the bed, where I was lying on my side, emotions in turmoil. "I don't know. You wanted this. You were happy about it. Proud."

"I didn't know it was going to be so hard then. I didn't know it would lead to this." My arms were covered, but he knew what I meant. I was fresh out of hospital—where the stress of university, and from simply being the emotionally unstable me, had landed me. "There's no point. I can't do this."

He put a hand on my hip. "There's no shame in quitting. If you can't do it, if you feel it's not right... It's all up to you. No one's going to judge you."

Maybe not, but I judged myself plenty enough. "If

I can't even finish a university course, then what else am I going to do?" Be a mess for the rest of my life, most likely.

"You've tried one thing, Josh. It wasn't the right thing for you, but that doesn't mean you give up." He rubbed my hip now, a soothing motion I recognised. It wasn't soothing me now though. "You tried something else. Maybe that'll fit you more. If not, you quit and try a third thing."

"Everyone knows what they want to do. Except me."

"No, Josh, not everyone knows. It's trial and error. Even if you wanted this before, doesn't mean you can't change your mind. Maybe I will too."

He was trying to make me feel better. It was sweet, but… "You won't." He was so certain, he did so well. He'd never change his mind. He'd last the course—and eventually he'd be a surgeon.

Me… well. I was a mess, and I always would be a mess. But at least I stumbled my way through it.

He was here for me, anyway.

So even if I did quit now, I'd be fine. I had him, and that was really all I needed. Though I did feel like an utter failure at the same time.

CHAPTER 24

The bed dipped and I blinked myself into the here and now. I turned over on my other side to find Damian's back sitting in front of me. He sighed.

I put my hand on the small of his back, hoping it would be of some comfort to him.

"Claire cannot afford to keep the house." His voice was low, not quite a whisper, but not far from it. "I'm in medical school. Chloe's a hairdresser. Neither of us can help her, not even put together." He propped his elbows on his knees and covered his face with his hands. "She wants to sell. I could quit school, get a job... then maybe she could keep it."

"No, Damian. No." He wanted to become a surgeon—he'd always known that. I wasn't going to let him quit now, when he was three years in and still so sure of his path. "If you, if they, want to keep the house, you can use my money. It's not like I'm using it. It's just sitting there in the bank."

"Not going to use your money, Josh."

"Why not?" I propped up on my elbow now. "If Claire, Matilda, and Matt want to stay here… I'll use it. It'll mean something then. I can't do anything—but I can do that. I mean, maybe I won't even have to. They've got life insurance and such, right, so I reckon she *could* keep the house if she absolutely wanted to."

He sighed again. "I don't even know if they want to stay."

Truthfully I wouldn't have wanted that. I didn't want to even be near the house if I had a choice. Not after Andrew had been here, after he'd hurt me here, sullied the place I'd always felt so good coming to. Just the thought of staying here any longer brought chills down my spine. Back when I was fifteen and Andrew was arrested, Mum had moved us out of the house and into a flat by the time I was out of hospital.

I'd never been more grateful for anything in my life. Going back to the house I only had terrible memories of… I couldn't have taken that.

Claire, Matilda, and Matt had good memories

from this house though… Except not anymore. Especially not Matt, who'd been the one who found me. What must it have been like for him? What must he have thought and felt?

"Talk to them. They might not want to stay here at all." Should I be truthful? I'd been living by that rule ever since I told Mum about Andrew. "I don't want to stay here. I've got good memories, but the last ones are not, and I just… I wouldn't want to stay."

He turned around slowly, gaze meeting mine, searching. "They've got a lot more good memories from here than you do. Matilda and Matthew grew up here. So did I." He turned away, sighing. His hands clasped together.

Of course. He didn't want Claire to lose the house, because this was his *home*. The home where he'd come after his family died, where he'd been safe, where he'd grown up to be the man he was today.

"Claire had no plan for this eventuality. Who thinks of something like this ever happening? You don't go around making plans for if your husband dies—" He stopped himself, took a deep breath. "How were any of us supposed to be ready for this?"

"You weren't." I sat up and leaned in close, resting against him. "No one can ever be prepared for something like this." I'd been expecting it—not

Ray dying, not ever that, but I'd been expecting Andrew—and *I* wasn't even prepared for it. Not even after ten years of abuse. Never prepared, never ready to deal with it, never ready to fight it.

"I didn't fight back," I whispered. "He overpowered me easily. I'm terrified of him. I'm not a kid anymore, but I am terrified. I didn't fight back."

His arm slid around me, pulling me in tighter. "Fear does that. It makes you freeze."

"It's pathetic. I'm twenty-one years old… I haven't got a lot going for me, but I should be able to fight back."

"He tormented you for ten years. As far as you can remember, he's been hurting you. Of course you're terrified of him. He used a little, defenseless kid. What you felt then… it's not going to go away in a blink of an eye." He squeezed me tight, cheek resting against the top of my head. "He's never coming near you again. He's going away for a long time now, and if when he does get out— if he decides to settle here in London again, then we'll move."

My heart started beating faster. "Yeah?" It was years ahead. I might be doing better then, whenever it happened, but that he put the possibility out there… it meant a lot.

"Yeah."

My nose rubbed against the side of his neck. "I love you so much."

"You too." Silence, then he drew a deep breath. "I never got to tell Ray how much he means to me. How much I appreciated all he's done for me. I don't think I ever, not even once, told him I love *him*."

He wasn't big with words, Damian. Not to anyone but me. I'd always required him speaking his feelings. Reassurance. Neediness, was what it was. "He knew." Ray wasn't—*hadn't been*—like me, doubting everything once there were no reassurance to be had. "Parent, or parental figures, they just know things like that. Trust me, Damian, he knew."

We hugged for a long time, no words spoken, just the two of us breathing in sync.

"Do you think they'll be all right?" he asked eventually.

I thought about it for a couple moments. "I hope so. Claire… it's hard to say. Matilda will be, I'm sure. Matt… I don't know." *Matt*. I wished it had been anyone but him who'd found me. Who'd come home to find the scene of the crash, to see the place his dad had died. No wonder he was locked up in his room, usually with his dog. No wonder he didn't eat, didn't cry, didn't speak. He must be in shock. "I think maybe therapy would be good for him." It had helped me, in any case, and Matt might be more like me than anyone realised.

He gave a brief nod. "Yeah. If he's willing. It's not like forcing him into would make anything better though."

That was true. I had been willing. Mum had got me into therapy right away—after I got out of hospital. There, therapy had been part of the deal, anyway. She had made sure, however, that I would continue once I was out. I'd been lucky—I'd met Vincent. I hadn't stopped going to therapy since. Not one-on-one with Vincent anyway. I'd dropped out of group therapy after Mal killed himself, though.

"I hope he's willing." I really did. Matt did need help—and I couldn't give it to him, no matter how much I knew what it was like to be traumatised. How much I knew cutting helped, though the scars it left would never go away. That they would be a symbol of shame, yet also a symbol of what I'd lived through.

I hoped Matt wouldn't inflict the kind of harm on himself that I'd done. I hoped whatever he'd dealt with before, coupled with recent events, wouldn't leave him as broken as I was.

I didn't want anyone to experience the way I was.

THE KITCHEN TABLE was decked out for all of us. And all of us were there, except I just— I couldn't.

"No." That table. The corner of it, my head, *blood*. I'd been in a coma for four days because Andrew had hit my head against it.

"Josh." Damian's arm clamped tight around my shoulders. "It's okay."

The doorbell rang shrilly.

Everyone seemed to stop, freeze up, for a second as the surprise washed over us. Matilda got up to answer the door, once it was clear no one else was moving anytime soon.

My gaze was already back on the table. On the corner. The corner that had left a hole in my head.

"Josh." Matilda came back. "It's your mum."

I glanced over at her briefly, but the table drew my attention like a magnet. It was impossible to resist.

"You need to come with me, Joshua."

Damian's arm tightened a bit more around my shoulders. "Where are you going?"

That's what I wonder too. Except my voice didn't work.

"To the police station."

"No!" I jerked out of Damian's half-hug. "No, I can't face him. Never again! No!" I shook my head wildly.

Mum glanced towards the table. "You're not going to, Joshua. You're not. You just have to tell the police what happened. It'll help."

Tell the police? *He killed Ray. He nearly killed you. Coma for four days...* My stomach sunk heavily. "He has to go to court again, hasn't he?"

I could see Claire tense up at the table. Matt had sunk so far down his chair it was a wonder he hadn't slid down onto the floor. Only Chloe and Matilda was paying rapt attention to Mum.

She nodded. "Yes. He committed a new crime. If —*when*—found guilty, the new sentence will be added onto the old one."

I closed my eyes. I didn't want to see any of them. I didn't want them to see *me*.

"Joshua, please. Come on. Don't make this harder on everyone."

I opened my eyes again to see Mum gazing at Claire. Claire was now the one with her eyes closed.

"Okay." I didn't want to argue, not here in front of all of them. They'd lost Ray. There was no doubt Andrew would get a new sentence—but seeing me fall apart because of a little chat with the police, of knowing I'd have to witness again in the future... that was not something I wanted them to see.

Damian squeezed my shoulder. "You want me to come with?"

I shook my head. "No, that's okay. You should stay here." I desperately wanted him to come. But I needed to not be so selfish. I needed to be able to do something by myself.

I trudged after Mum outside.

"They've wanted to talk to you ever since you woke up in the hospital, but I put them off." She got in the driver's seat.

I slid into the passenger seat. "I don't want to stand in that witness box again."

"I'm afraid you'll have to." She started the car and backed slowly out of the driveway. The same way Andrew must've done when he'd hurried to get away from his crime scene—only he'd gone a lot faster. And he'd crashed right into Ray. "You do want to put him away, don't you?"

"Yes. Of course." But I didn't want to see him. Didn't want to see those cold eyes with no remorse. He wasn't just this evil person I'd made him out to be in my mind—he truly *was* evil. There was nothing at all redemptive about him. Not a single thing. No matter what he'd experienced in his life, no matter what left him the monster he was, I felt no compassion. None at all. "Why can't *he* just die?"

Mum's fingers tightened on the steering wheel. "Because the world's unfair."

"He got away with no injuries?"

"Just some whiplash, as far as I could gather."

Figures.

"You'll get through this too, Joshua." She reached over to pat my hand tentatively. "You've got through so much already. This'll be nothing. Besides, you know legal procedures don't exactly come around quickly, so it'll be a while until another court case."

Yes, I had got through a lot. But I was a right mess too. *Still alive though. That's something.*

"I don't want to do this."

"I know." She sighed. "I don't want to make you do this. But you have to. They need to hear what happened from you."

Yeah. I knew I had to. I knew it would help. Maybe he'd get another year or two for what he did to me along with what he'd get for killing Ray.

Still didn't mean I wanted to do this.

*C*hristmas.

The most festive time of the year. Or so they said. I'd never been fond of it. It had never brought me any good.

Last year I'd been hospitalised through the whole of December. This year, though, I was going to celebrate with my boyfriend—and my mum and his aunt and uncle. My mum's girlfriend, Claire's sister, as well as Damian's cousins, too.

For once in my life, I didn't dread Christmas.

Claire and Harriet were in the kitchen, preparing the food. The kids were in the living room watching the telly. The rest of us were seated on the dining table. It was all decked out, ready for food consumption.

"Need help carrying anything?" Ray raised his voice so he'd be heard in the kitchen.

"Yes, please!"

Ray nodded to himself and rose. Mum and Damian made to rise as well, but Ray motioned for them to sit back down before disappearing through the kitchen doorway.

Soon the table was filled and everyone sat at it. It looked and smelled so good my mouth practically watered.

I glanced to my side, at mum. She was sitting next to Harriet—and as I looked they smiled at each other, the kind of wide, happy smile of people who were in love and liked to be in each other's company.

Claire was speaking to the kids, while Ray looked on and smiled to himself. Chloe was piling her plate with hot food.

I looked at Damian. He was already looking at me. And there was a small smile there, the ones usually reserved for me. And now I was smiling, because his smile meant the world to me. It meant he was happy, content, that he still wanted me around.

I wanted to be here. With them, celebrating every holiday. I wanted to be a part of this, of them.

The two Christmases before hadn't been good either. I'd ended up hospitalised during both, so mum and I had never had the chance of actually enjoying it once Andrew was out of our lives.

Christmas was the hardest to deal with of it all. We'd hardly ever celebrated with the rest of the family down in Bristol. Mum being off from work had meant that Andrew turned even sneakier—and nastier.

I hated Christmas.

But now... I might actually grow fond of it.

CHAPTER 25

I went home afterwards.

I was exhausted and going back to face Ray and Claire's house was not something I was up to.

"Hey." Silver was home when I got there. He was sprawled over the smaller sofa, surfing through channels on the TV.

"Hi." I sank down on the other sofa.

He eyed me. "How are you feeling?"

I shrugged. "I'm going to stay here tonight." I wanted to go be with Damian, but... I couldn't face that house. I couldn't face all of them. "I think it'll be best if he gets some alone-time with them. That he doesn't have to worry about me."

"Have you let him know? Or else I'll promise you, he'll be worried."

"Yeah, I sent him a text earlier." After I got out of the police station and told Mum to drive me home. She hadn't come up with me because I'd insisted *she* go home. There'd been light in the flat, which meant someone was home, so she'd relented a lot easier than she normally would've. I wasn't about to do anything while Silver and Kian were around, anyway.

"Good." He nodded, then turned back to the telly where he switched channels again. "There's nothing on. Tell you what, how about we rent a film and order in? Have a nice, quiet evening in front of the telly?"

A smile spread on my lips. It was small, but a smile nonetheless. "That sounds great." Just what I needed. Get my mind off everything.

The door rattled, opened, and then Kian came spilling inside. "Hi!" He smiled once he spotted Silver, then again as he saw me. "Josh! What a surprise."

"We're ordering in. Watching a film." Silver tilted his head back to get a more proper look at Kian. "It's just the three of us and we're going to have a nice, quiet evening."

"Now that I like the sound of." Kian strode over

and bent to press a light kiss to Silver's lips.

They had such a different relationship than Damian and I had. Every time I saw them interact, I couldn't help but think about it. They were so loving, so intimate… it was always what I'd wished for, but once I met Damian— being like that wasn't something he was comfortable with. Constantly touching, kissing, sex… it was not for him. And I liked what we had. I was happy. Well, as happy as I *could* be.

My phone vibrated.

I pulled it up from my pocket. Damian had answered my text.

Damian: OK. You all right?

I wasn't surprised he worried.

Me: Yeah, I'm fine. S, K, and I are ordering in and watching a film.

I waited anxiously for his answer. It popped in not long after.

Damian: Have fun! See you tomorrow.

My fingers tapped on the screen without thought, writing 'you too'. Then I stopped myself. I couldn't encourage him to have *fun*. Nothing was fun for him right now. Definitely not staying over in that house, without his uncle. Knowing Ray was dead.

Instead I wrote something else.

Me: I love you.

Damian: Love you too.

With nothing more to say, I hesitantly put my phone at my side, screen facing down. I chewed my lip, worried. "I have no idea what's going to happen now," I murmured, without thought.

"No one knows what's going to happen in the future." Kian clapped my shoulder on his way past. "What happens, happens. No need to worry about it before you have to. I'm taking a shower!"

Silver caught my gaze. "I know things suck right now. And it feels like they aren't going to get any better. But they will. Eventually. A bit better, anyway."

First then did I remember that Silver had lost someone. His boyfriend and two best friends. In a car crash—where he'd driven the car. He'd been the only survivor.

Even Kian, no matter his cheerful attitude most of the time, had baggage. He had a mum who had neglected him his entire childhood. Who'd kept his dad, who wanted to be a part of his life, away.

Everyone had baggage—and most people lived through it. For most people, it got better. It would for me too. For us. Hopefully. *Damian's lost so many people already. He's not going to lose me. I'll make sure of that.* Easy enough to promise, not that easy to maintain. But I'd do my best. I'd take my meds, go to therapy, maybe even start back up with group, if Vincent felt it would help. Anything not to spiral back down and do something impulsive again...

Damian didn't deserve more heartbreak. He had enough already. His whole family dead now... his only actual blood relatives left were Matilda and Matt. *Matt...* Who knew what went on with him? What would happen to him.

"Hey." Silver's hand clamped onto my knee. He'd bent forward and was now staring intensely at me. "Let it go for one night, okay? Let's enjoy our evening. You're allowed to, you know, to enjoy your-self. So, whatever's bothering you, put it away for a few hours. For the whole night, preferably." He smiled slightly, but it wasn't a happy smile.

The one I returned wasn't happy either.

But at least it was a smile. At least I was capable of it.

It was something.

CHAPTER 26

The house was empty. Floors and walls were bare, the windows devoid of curtains and flowers; everything that had made it a home. The contents had been sold or thrown away or put in storage. A few possessions had come with them to their new flat, like most of the furniture from both Matilda and Matt's rooms, as well as pictures and knick-knacks of sentimental value.

Claire hadn't wanted to keep much of the bigger stuff. It was too painful for her. Like their bed. She couldn't bring herself to throw it or sell it, so she'd put it in storage, and bought a new one for herself.

I could totally understand.

Damian walked from room to room. He left the basement til last. I followed him down without a word. He hadn't spoken since we entered the house, and I didn't want to break the silence.

Once inside his old room, Damian stopped. Right in the middle of it. He looked around, eyes filling with tears. I could see he tried to stop them, but he was unsuccessful. They spilled over, running down his cheeks.

"They had two toddlers to take care of," he whispered in a broken voice. "Yet they came to the hospital the second they were notified. They took me home—and I stayed there until Silver and I moved into the flat. They didn't even hesitate." He wiped furiously at the tears. "I came here from an abusive childhood, to people who wanted me, who were *normal*. I'd never known that before. No more fits of anger, of being slapped around, of emotional abuse. I was safe here. They made it safe. For the first time… Only good things happened to me after they took me in, and now Ray's not here anymore to see what good they both did for me."

I walked up behind him and wrapped my arms around his waist, leaning against his back, resting my cheek against the top of his spine. "He knew. He knew how much you loved them all and he knew what he'd done for you, how much you appreciated it. He knew you were going to be okay, that you *were* okay."

"They worried about me, you know. Until you came along."

They'd worried Damian would forever be alone. He'd had no interest in anyone—except me. Here I was, three years on, and we were still together.

"My family's gone. Ray is gone. Now the house is gone too. It's too bloody much." He drew a shaky breath and that simple motion seemed to tip the full glass over. He turned abruptly, a sob escaped him as he wrapped his arms around my shoulders and cried into my neck.

I stood steady, held him tight, and let him let it loose.

"I don't know what I'd do without you." His voice was hoarse, broken, wounded.

"Me neither." I clung to him, needing his strength as much as he needed mine. "What was it Silver said back when me met? *'Maybe two scarred souls can make each other whole'*. I think he was right. As whole as we could be, anyway."

He didn't reply, only cried on, but I knew he'd heard me because he held onto me tighter.

"Do you think the house was sold too soon? If you can't handle it—"

He drew back and wiped at his eyes. "It's fine. I'm fine. I can." He looked around at the empty, hollow room again. "This was always my room. Even when I moved out, they left it exactly as it'd been when I still lived here."

"They love you so much." Loved, in Ray's case. I ran my hand over his face.

His gaze settled on me, who in turn was studying him closely. He looked a right mess, all cried-out, eyes red and sore. He'd seen me like that so often— but I could count on one hand how many times I'd seen him like this.

He cupped my cheek fondly. "I love you so much. I try to tell you often, but I don't think I'm very good at it."

I smiled widely. "I love you too." My fingers wrapped loosely around his wrist. "And you are. Good at it, I mean. You're amazing." No one else would be able to keep up with me and my mood swings. His patience... it was legendary. "Are you ready to go? I've got something for you at home."

He looked around again. "Yeah." He entwined his fingers with min. "I'm ready."

FOUR MONTHS AGO

*D*amian's shoulder pressed against mine as we watched the fireworks light up the sky.

Ray stood further forward, preparing a firework together with Matt. Claire and Matilda were at Damian's side. Matilda also watched the sky, whereas Claire kept glancing ahead, a bit worried.

Mum was at my other side, along with Harriet. She met my gaze as I glanced at her and I swear I saw her give a small smile, though it was hard to see in the dark.

I smiled anyway, leaning further against Damian.

He turned his head to look at me.

"Feeling all right?"

I nodded quickly. "Yeah."

"Good." He bumped our foreheads together gently.

Another firework went off, and I could see the bright lilac colour reflected in Damian's blue eyes.

For once, my arms didn't hurt because I'd attacked them with a razor. I didn't feel all bleak, and miserable, and vulnerable. For once I felt calm. I felt good. I felt loved.

All these people… they loved me. Front and centre was Damian. My heart seemed to swell just from looking at him.

"I love you." I did. With all my heart. Even when I was in a fit, when I was so far down I couldn't see anything good— I never stopped loving him.

He gave me a flicker of a smile. "I love you too."

I wanted to kiss him—I almost did—but we were surrounded by people. That he was here with me, forehead resting against mine, had to be enough for now. It was enough. It would always be enough—not a bit more intimacy wouldn't be amiss either. It wouldn't happen while we were amongst other people though.

And I was okay with that.

Because that was him. That was how he worked. And somehow—though I'd never thought it would— it worked for me too.

As long as we were together, I'd be fine with anything. Because we did work.

We worked really well together.

"*I* started a blog," I told him.

Matilda's suggestion had been going round and round in my mind, all kinds of intriguing, and I'd finally acted on it.

"An online blog. Instead of handwritten journals, I'll be typing everything from now on. Sharing. There's a lot of people like me out there. A lot of people who struggle with all kinds of things. It's nice too, to get my feelings down in writing again."

I fumbled with my tablet, looking for the other thing, the one I wanted to show him. "I also sort of wrote a book."

He glanced at me. "You *sort of* wrote a book? How does that work exactly?"

I chuckled, all kinds of self-conscious. "It's not

finished yet. It's only half-way there, but— I did. I wrote it. It's fiction, but drawn on a lot of my, um, experiences. I guess that makes it kind of autobiographical. I was thinking of maybe trying to get it published, but I don't know… it's kind of personal." I wrung my hands, the tablet resting on my knees now. All I had to do was press my finger on the book and it would open. "I do want you to read through what I've got though. You're the only person I *need* to read this book."

I pressed the cover. It wasn't so much a cover, as just a standard background with the title, but if I did try to get it published, I'd have to look into that. "Here."

Damian took it once I handed it over, glancing at me, then down at the screen. And he stared at it. I knew what was there, what was getting to him.

Scarred Souls
An autobiographical novel
Joshua Slater

"Silver's words." Silver had mentioned them to Damian, but once Damian had told me I'd never been able to get them out of my head. "It fits us so well. We're scarred, both of us, outside and inside." I drew my lower lip in between my teeth, biting down gently. "Turn the page."

He pressed his finger to the corner of the screen, which caused the paper to flip over to the next page. It was the dedication page, and now he stared even more, unblinking as he let the words sink in. They might be simple words, and a bit cliché, but I meant them with all my heart.

> *Damian—*
> *This one is for you,*
> *The love of my life.*
> *We will always be together.*
> *I love you—*
> *Josh*

He put the tablet down and instead turned to me. His fingers tangled in my hair and he tugged me gently towards him. "I love you too. So much. I don't know what I would've done lately without you."

I smoothed my hand down his cheek, jaw, and down his neck. "You and me," I whispered, leaning in closer. "Always."

He leaned in all the way for the kiss.

"That sounds like a perfect plan."

ABOUT THE AUTHOR

TT lives in Norway and writes about gay men living in Norway. She also occasionally writes about gay men living in the UK, because she loves the UK. Norway might be too cold for her, but TT doesn't like the summer, so she's learned to adapt. TT is happiest in front of her computer, creating emotional stories about men loving other men.

www.ttkove.com
ttkove@gmail.com